SHIVER

Night Roamers

(Book Two)

By Kristen Middleton

To:

My loving family, awesome friends, and all of the wonderful people who continue to support me.

Thank You...

Prologue

Hip hop music pulsated throughout the dark club as Ashley followed Jenny through its crowd of undulating bodies. Both girls were heading towards the bar where Jenny was set on buying her first "Sex on the Beach" using her new fake driver's license. Both seventeen-year-olds had received them from "Creepy" Curt Hammer before seventh period gym class the day before. Curt could get anything and everything you needed.

For a price.

His price wasn't yet known to the girls, but his presence at the club tonight would be certain. He'd practically begged them to show.

"Don't forget to meet me outside of the V.I.P. lounge at Club Nightshade, ten o'clock," he'd reminded them as they were leaving Jenny's locker earlier in the day.

Jenny had gushed with excitement. "Are you freakin' serious, Curt? How in the hell did someone like *you* pull that off?"

"Let's just say I have friends in high places," he'd replied with a tight smile.

Nightshade was a brand new club that had opened in Shore Lake. Everyone at school was hyped about it. Tuesdays were officially "Teen Night", but weekends were supposed to be off the hook. If you could find a way to get in, you'd have the chance to experience some really intense partying. Now, it was almost ten o'clock as Ashley held onto Jenny's belt loop, trying not to lose her friend through the tangle of bodies. Before they cleared the packed crowd, however, someone grabbed her by the elbow, forcing her to stop, breaking her connection with Jenny.

"Jenny!" she called to her friend, who was already disappearing through the rowdy crowd.

"Hey, sweet-thing, how about a dance?" a deep voice rasped into her ear.

She turned towards the guy and swallowed. *Scary.*

His bald head was covered with skull tattoos and he had a single silver ball pierced just below his bottom lip. His breath reeked of liquor and something more pungent than cigarettes.

She stepped back and swallowed. "Um...no, but thanks, anyway."

He scowled. "Why not? You think you're too special or something?"

She shook her head, vehemently. "No... please... I'm just trying to follow my friend."

"Your loss," he grunted.

Very doubtful, she thought, noticing the long, ragged scar under his chin. He was definitely trouble.

Ashley turned around and pushed through more bodies until she reached Jenny, who was already at the bar.

"Oh, there you are. I ordered for you," said Jenny, her eyes sparkling with excitement.

Ashley flipped her dark hair over her shoulder and smiled. "Okay, thanks."

"What happened to you? I thought I'd lost you," she asked.

"Some guy tried asking me to dance," replied Ashley.

Jenny's eyes lit up. "Was he hot?"

Before Ashley could answer, the guy in question parked himself onto the stool right next to them.

"This seat taken?" he asked with an arrogant smile.

Jenny shrugged. "Actually, we aren't staying, so you can do whatever you want with it."

He took a swig of his beer. "Why not? I bet you could use some company."

"We're *not* looking for it," Jenny replied.

He smiled coldly. "You know, it isn't safe in a club like this for two little girls such as yourselves. It can be pretty dangerous if you're not careful."

The bartender interrupted before either girl could respond. He slid their drinks across the bar and said, "Drinks are on the house. Also, the V.I.P. is upstairs. They're waiting for you."

Jenny and Ashley looked at each other and smiled in delight. Not only had they scored big in getting into the nightclub, but they were also guests in the V.I.P. lounge.

It was, a dream come true.

"That guy was a *total* loser," whispered Jenny as he finally took the hint and moved towards another conquest, a bleached blond cougar, sitting alone at the other end of the bar.

Ashley nodded, relieved that he'd moved on. Something had been really off about that guy, making her skin crawl.

Jenny took a sip of her drink and motioned for Ashley to follow her up the stairs. When they reached the top, Curt was standing outside of what appeared to be a private room.

"Good, you made it," he said, looking at little tense.

"Hell yeah we made it," replied Jenny, taking another drink of her cocktail. "We wouldn't miss this for the world."

"Lead the way, Jenny," said Curt, waving her in.

"Don't mind if I do," she said, stepping through the entrance.

"Mm…you're looking really hot, Ashley," murmured Curt.

She shivered as his beady eyes raked over her tight shimmery black dress. "Well, ah…thanks, Curt."

His eyes stared unabashedly at her cleavage. "After you," he said, holding the door open.

She stepped past him and entered the dimly lit room where Jenny was already making herself comfortable on a plush, black leather sectional.

"Wow," said Ashley. Having never been in any club before, let alone a V.I.P. lounge, she was impressed. There were several tall glass tables set up near a large plate window overlooking the dance floor, a video game area, and a long bar in which a totally hot bartender was busy cleaning cocktail glasses. As if sensing her interest, he looked up and flashed a ten-thousand-watt smile, making her blush.

"This place is fucking awesome," declared Jenny, her eyes already shining from the alcohol.

"That it is," murmured Curt, looking at a message on his phone. "So, something just came up, girls, and I've got to split."

"Okay, well, thanks for everything, Curt," said Ashley, relieved he wasn't staying. The way he stared at her body made her feel dirty.

He nodded. "You bet."

"So, is there going to be a party here or something?" asked Jenny. "I mean, we're not going to be the only ones in the V.I.P. lounge, right?"

"Oh, you could say there's going to be a party," he replied with a small smile. "In fact, tonight's a private party and you two girls are the honored guests."

Jenny raised her eyebrows. "Seriously? That's kind of weird, though, isn't it? I mean, we've never even been here before tonight."

"That's okay," called Curt, walking towards the exit. "You're young, hot, and tasty. It's all good."

"He's so weird," whispered Ashley after he'd left.

Jenny smirked. "That's why he's called 'Creepy' Curt."

A new song by "Pink" blasted through the club and Ashley was dying to dance.

"I think we should go back downstairs," she said, biting the side of her lip. "Wasn't the point of coming here to check out guys and dance our asses off?"

Before Jenny could respond, the door opened and a dark-haired guy wearing a long, black leather coat entered the lounge.

"Oh, hi," said Jenny, standing up.

"Ladies," murmured the devilishly handsome stranger. "Welcome to Club Nightshade."

Ashley could hardly breathe. The guy was tall with broad shoulders and full lips. As he stared into her eyes with his crystal blue ones, a fire ignited between her legs.

"Hi," she answered, breathlessly.

"Hi," said Jenny, who was also mesmerized by the stranger's hypnotic stare. "Who are you?"

He licked his lips and smiled. "I'll be your host tonight. My name is Ethan."

Chapter One

"Excuse me, waitress, can I get another coffee over here?" snapped the twenty-something blond with the Bluetooth attached to her ear. She'd been sitting in the corner of the diner, talking loudly into the headset, making sure everyone around her knew she was important. From her boasting, I understood she was some type of investor, and a successful one at that. To me, she'd been nothing but a royal bitch.

"Are you ready to order yet?" I asked quietly, refilling her cup of coffee for the fourth time. She'd been in the diner for almost an hour and I'd tried to take her order several times, in which she'd brushed me away with her hand like a bothersome fly.

This time she gave me an arrogant smile. "Yes, waitress ... I'd like the Oriental Chicken Salad."

Bitch.

I looked up from my order pad. "Excuse me?"

The woman raised her eyebrows. "I'm sorry?"

I could have sworn I heard her say "bitch", and from the smug look on her face, it seemed very likely.

"Sorry, I thought I heard you say something else," I mumbled.

She looked at her watch. "I just gave you my order and I don't have much time to wait."

Get moving, Bimbo...

This time I'd been staring at the woman, and her lips hadn't moved when she'd called me a "Bimbo", but I'd heard it as clear as day.

Stunned, I stepped backwards, right into Susan, knocking her tray over. "Oh, God! I'm sorry, Susan!" I groaned in horror, my face turning red.

Susan bent down and began picking up the water glasses. "It's fine, Nikki. Fortunately, it wasn't anything important," she replied. "Just a little water."

As I bent down to help Susan, the evil blond customer's voice popped into my head once again.

What a dumb, stupid bitch.

I stood up and stared at her. "What did you just call me?"

Her eyes narrowed. "I don't know what in the hell you're talking about."

"Having problems over here?" asked Rosie, coming towards us.

"Sorry," I mumbled. "My fault, I bumped into Susan."

"Don't sweat it, honey," said Rosie. "It's just water. I'll help you, Susan. Nikki, go and seat those other people who just walked in."

"Can somebody place *my* damn order?" snapped the woman, tapping her long, painted nails against the table. "I don't have a lot of time here."

"Certainly," I replied.

"Don't worry, Nikki. I'll just seat the new customers," said Susan.

Jesus, is everyone around here incompetent twits?

I turned back to the woman and scowled.

"Let me guess, you already forgot what I ordered?" she asked with a tight smile.

I smiled coldly. "No. I was just going to suggest the House Salad. It takes less time to make and fewer calories than the Oriental."

Her mouth opened. "What in the hell is that supposed to mean?"

I shrugged and gave her an innocent look. "I'm just saying... you're in a hurry. The extra calories in the salad dressing might bog you down."

Her eyes narrowed. "Just order me the fucking Oriental Salad."

"Excuse me," interrupted Rosie. "Ma'am, that's no way to talk to one of my waitresses."

The woman reached into her purse and threw a couple of dollar bills onto the table. "You know what?" she huffed. "Screw this two-bit diner. I don't have time for this bullshit." Then she slid out of the booth and stomped out of the restaurant.

Rosie shook her head. "I'm not sure what that was all about, but sometimes, it's just better to let customers like that leave."

"I'm sorry," I said to her. "It was probably my fault."

"No," said Susan. "Don't be so hard on yourself. That's just Faye Dunbar and everyone knows she's an annoying cunt."

My jaw dropped and I burst out laughing.

"I have to agree with you there, Susie," chuckled Rosie. "Spoiled rich girl with some major superiority issues."

I wiped away my tears and then went to go check back on my other customers, trying hard to forget about Faye. I still wasn't sure how I was able to read her mind, but I knew it wasn't my imagination and that the words had come directly from her.

"I just seated an old friend of yours," murmured Susan, coming up behind me as I refilled one of the coffeemakers with water.

"Really?"

I looked over towards my section and felt a pang of regret.

Duncan.

We hadn't spoken in over three months; his choice, unfortunately, not mine. He hadn't gotten over the night I'd disappeared with Ethan, if only to say goodbye. It had been very willingly on my part, even after Duncan and my brother had basically rescued me from Ethan's house of vampires. When all was said and done, nobody believed that Ethan or the others were, in fact, vampires. Not even my brother, Nathan. He'd somehow been brainwashed to forget. I knew without a doubt that Caleb, my mother's boyfriend, A.K.A. town sheriff, A.K.A. head vampire, certainly had a hand in that. With the power of persuasion, he could pretty much control anyone's mind he wanted. That is, except for mine. Somehow, I was now immune to it. My only guess was that it had something to do with Ethan sinking his teeth into my neck before he'd left town. He'd been weak and I'd offered to let him feed before leaving for New York.

And feed he had, almost to the point of my death.

At least, that's what Caleb had told me. Luckily for me, Caleb and my mother had arrived while Ethan was still attached to my neck, draining the blood from my body. My mom had freaked out and Caleb had shot Ethan, sending him away like a ghost in the night. Now Caleb and I had an understanding; I wouldn't talk and he'd protect my family from the other vampires.

"Hi," I said, stopping by Duncan's table. He was with his dad, Sonny, and looked like he wanted to take off as soon as I approached.

"Well, hello, Nikki," smiled Sonny.

Duncan nodded but focused most of his attention on the menu, which hurt. I realized right then and there that I still had feelings for him and would have done almost anything to at least have his friendship.

I cleared my throat. "Um, can I get you something to drink?"

"Coffee for me," said Sonny. "What about you, Dunc?"

"Just water," he said, still trying to avoid my eyes.

"Okay," I said.

"Your brother is doing a fine job at the marina," said Sonny, rapping his knuckles on the table. "Yep, a fine job. He's a hard worker."

I nodded. "Yeah, he must be doing something because he's completely wiped out when he gets home," I said.

onny smiled. "We keep him hopping. But ⸳ms to like it even so."

I nodded. "He says he loves it."

"So, how's your mom doing?" asked Sonny. "I heard she was having some problems with her eyes?"

Duncan glanced at me when I answered. "Yeah, she still does. She's been to a couple of specialists, but they don't really know what it is."

Secretly I knew, though. Caleb was slowly turning my mother into a vampire. I'm not sure exactly when the final change was going to happen and he claimed that he was only doing it to save her from cancer. What I did know was that she hadn't been given a choice about becoming a vampire, and she scoffed at me when I tried to talk to her about it. She believed that I was watching too many late night movies and they were going to my head.

"Well, hopefully it will clear up. Just tell her I said hello and that the offer still stands to get her out on my boat."

"I will," I said.

I left to give them time to look over the menus. After refilling coffees and checking on the status of my other orders, I went back to their table and realized that Duncan was missing. Sonny explained that he had some errands to run and had realized he didn't have time to eat.

"That's too bad," I said.

Sonny nodded. "Ever since he started hanging out with Caleb's daughter, he's been up late and moving slow during the day. I just don't know what's gotten into that boy."

My throat went dry. "He's been hanging out with Celeste?"

Sonny took a sip of coffee. "Yeah. Says they're just friends, but the way she looks at him, he's got to be blind if he doesn't see it."

I felt a pang of jealousy mixed with fear. I highly doubted her intentions were good. "How long have they been hanging out?"

"Oh, about a month now. Pretty girl she is, but a little on the wild side."

Wild side? He had no idea.

I only nodded.

"Anyway, I suppose I'd better order. I'll have The Special," he said, looking into his menu, "with my eggs over easy, please."

I nodded. "Sounds good, Sonny."

He looked at me. "You know, I'm surprised I haven't seen you around the marina lately."

I shrugged. "I know. Now that school's started and I've been working here at the diner, I haven't had time to do much of anything else."

"Well, pity. I think Duncan was beginning to really like you."

I stared out the window, noticing in dismay that Duncan was standing in the parking lot talking to Celeste. She was sitting in her truck,

..ick, dark sunglasses and a pouty
..ion. She must have sensed I was watching,
..use she turned towards me and smiled.

It gave me the chills.

"Nikki?"

I looked at Sonny. "I'm sorry, what did you say?"

He chuckled. "Nothing, don't worry about it."

"Nikki, one of your orders is up," said Rosie, passing by the table. "Hey, Sonny."

"Hi, Rosie."

I left Sonny's table and finished up my shift, thinking about Duncan and Celeste.

What in the hell did she really want with him?

Whatever it was, it made me nervous. I decided it was about time to hash everything out with Duncan, whether he liked it or not.

Chapter Two

"Where's mom?" I asked, walking through the door. It was after ten o'clock and my arches were killing me. I took off my shoes and began rubbing the soles of my feet.

Nathan was sitting on the couch eating a large bowl of cookie dough ice cream. "I think she's at Caleb's again," he said between bites. "How's the car running?"

I shrugged. "It's running, okay. It kind of hesitated when I started it tonight, though."

"Hmm... I'll take a look at it tomorrow. It might just need an oil change."

My mom had graciously loaned me the money for a used Camaro she'd spotted in town last month, when I'd turned eighteen. It had

ಲ work but thankfully, Nathan knew
ುout engines to make it drivable. With
ಲ and scratches, it wasn't the most
ಲtive vehicle, but it got me where I needed to

"Thanks," I said.

"You going out tonight?" he asked, standing up.

I shook my head. "No, I'm too tired."

Plus, it wasn't like I'd had made a lot of friends in school as of yet. There were a couple of girls I sat with at lunch, but after what happened last summer and the things going on with my mom, I still had a hard time getting close to anyone.

"Okay, well I'm going out with Duncan and Celeste later. If you need anything, you have my cell phone."

My jaw dropped. "You're actually hanging out with Celeste, too?"

He nodded. "Yeah, she's a nice girl. Plus, she has some really hot girlfriends."

I looked at him incredulously. "She's a freakin' vampire, Nathan! I can't believe you don't remember anything that happened last summer with Ethan. Celeste was involved with all of that, you know."

His face darkened. "Ethan was just a loser who wouldn't take 'no' for an answer. You know, you're starting to really scare me with all of this vampire talk, Nikki. Jesus, don't you know how ridiculous you sound?"

"Listen to me, Nathan! Celeste is dangerous and so are her friends. I wish you'd believe me."

He snorted. "The only thing dangerous about Celeste is her choice in clothes, which," he said with a devilish grin, "is dangerously sexy."

"You're so naïve," I mumbled.

He laughed. "For the love of God, Nikki! Celeste is *Caleb's* daughter. You know, the sheriff; mom's boyfriend? Jesus, we're practically family now."

I scowled. "Don't even go there. We are not family and never will be. Caleb and Celeste are both vampires, and the sooner you realize that, the safer we'll all be."

He waved his hand in exasperation and started walking up the steps towards his bedroom. "I don't have time for this. You obviously need help."

That hurt. My twin brother didn't believe me, probably thought I was a total nutcase, and there was nothing I could do to persuade him otherwise. Feeling overwhelmingly defeated, I decided to take a shower and go to bed. I was tired, crabby, and totally on my own for the night. After grabbing an apple from the kitchen, I went upstairs to my bedroom and turned on the television. The news was on and the story being covered left me totally breathless.

ʒenaged girls' bodies were discovered
ds early this morning near Bearpaw
private beach located in southern Shore
said the young woman, standing outside of
Sheriff's Department. "The girls, Ashley
ᴄaruthers and Jenny Friedley, both longtime
friends and seniors at Shore Lake High School,
were last seen by their parents shortly before nine
o'clock Friday night. Although officials are not
commenting on the condition of the bodies, foul
play is suspected. Unfortunately, no other
information is being released at this time. Back to
you, Jim."

I stared at the screen in horror. Ashley and
Jenny were two of the most popular girls in school.
They also had a reputation for partying with
college students and sneaking into trashy bars.
Even with that, however, there was no doubt in my
mind of what kind of evil befell them.

Vampires.

Nathan stuck his head into my room as I
turned off the television. "Later, Twerp."

I looked at him, unable to form any words.

His lips thinned. "Okay, what's wrong?"

I cleared my throat. "Ashley Caruthers and
Jenny Friedley were both found murdered," I said,
my voice hollow.

He eyes widened. "You're shitting me?"

I shook my head and sat down on the bed. "Their bodies were found near Bearpaw Cove. They think it's foul play."

"I wonder if Caleb will give us any more details," he said, running a hand through his brown hair. "That's just crazy. They seemed like nice girls, although I heard they liked to party pretty hard; must have caught up with them."

Nice wasn't the word I'd used to describe Jenny. Ashley was friendly, enough, but Jenny was a total snob. Or, rather, she used to be.

Nathan's phone began to ring and he answered it. From the goofy grin on his face, I could tell it was a girl. He stepped out of my room to talk in private then returned after a few minutes.

"Listen, I've gotta fly; you going to be okay?"

I nodded.

The truth was that I was more worried about him than anything. Hanging out with a vampire whose intentions were probably not in his best interests didn't sit well with me. The only thing keeping me from going totally insane was Caleb's promise to keep Nathan and my mom safe. I hoped that included being unharmed by Celeste.

He walked over and planted a kiss on the top of my head. "Don't let this thing drive you crazy," he said. "Obviously, those two got themselves in over their heads with someone or ho knows, maybe they were into

y eyes narrowed. "Or maybe…"

"Don't even say it," he interrupted.

I folded my hands under my chest. "Why on't you ever believe me?"

He threw up his hands in exasperation. "Because there are no such things as monsters, werewolves, or vampires. You have to wake up. Whoever got to these girls is just some sick fuck that needs to be locked up. Hopefully, Caleb can stop whoever's doing this shit before anything else happens."

I rolled my eyes. "Caleb, right."

"Caleb's a good guy and you just keep ripping him to shreds. Look, I'm finished with this conversation. Keep the doors locked and call me if you need me."

"Fine," I mumbled, looking away.

Nathan stared at me like he wanted to shake some sense into me. In the end, he just left me alone to sulk.

Chapter Three

After I took a shower, I went downstairs to the den for something to read. With an entire library of books nestled in the pine cabinets, I had more than enough choices to help get my mind off of my own horrific realities. As I went down the various rows, I came across a nonfiction book about vampires.

"See, Nathan," I muttered. "There is a book written about vampires. It's even a nonfictional book."

I brought the book upstairs into my bedroom and collapsed onto the bed. As I began reading about Dracula or Vlad Tepes, a.k.a. "Vlad the Impaler", my lids grew heavy and soon, I drifted off to sleep.

***

"Nikki," said Jenny. "Hurry up."

"I'm trying," I said, following her into the dark club. I was wearing spiked heels and wobbled like a young doe. "Where's Ashley?"

Her eyes sparkled as she looked back at me. "She's waiting for us."

"Where is everyone?" I called.

"Hurry up, slow poke, they are waiting for us."

Everyone was waiting for us?

I thought that was strange, but then so was the fact that I was wearing stilettos.

"This way," urged Jenny, still far ahead of me.

We walked downstairs to a long hallway. At the end of it was a large door. Jenny pushed it open and I followed her inside.

"What is this place?" I whispered.

A group of people were gathered around something in the center of the room.

"Let's go," said Jenny, pushing through the crowd while I hesitated. Something was wrong; I felt it in my gut.

"Come on, Nikki!" called Jenny, disappearing.

I swallowed my fear and pushed through the crowd. When I made it to the center, the blood rushed to my ears.

"Hi," said the girl lying naked on the bed. Her throat was cut and blood trickled down her neck.

"Ashley?" I whispered in horror.

She lifted her head, exposing more of her wound. "What do you think?" she asked.

"What do you mean?"

She smiled dreamily. "Do you think he'll like it?"

I shook my head, confused. "Who?"

"Him," she said, looking behind me.

I turned around and gasped in surprise as my eyes locked with the vampire's. "Ethan?"

***

A warm breath whispered into my ear, "Nikki..."

I gasped and sat up, pulling my blankets around my shoulders. When I realized I'd been dreaming, I let out a shaky sigh and looked at my alarm clock.

It was after two a.m.

I stretched my legs and yawned, then got up to use the bathroom. When I was finished, I flicked off my lights and got back into bed, prepared to sleep until late in the morning. Just as I was drifting off, I heard a soft thump. When I opened my eyes, a shadow moved across my balcony.

Oh, my God!

I leaped out of bed and raced out of my bedroom, hysterical with terror. As I rushed downstairs to grab a knife or something to defend myself, the front door opened and Nathan walked in with Celeste.

"Nathan!" I choked. "Thank God you're home!'

"What's wrong?" he asked, moving towards me, his eyes full of concern.

"Someone was on my balcony!" I said, pointing upstairs.

Before I could stop him, Nathan bounded up the stairs to investigate.

"I'm sure it's nothing," said Celeste, a small smile on her face.

I glared at her. "It's probably one of your bloodsucking friends. Why don't you go and help him!"

She looked at me with amusement. "My...my...my... I see someone's a little paranoid."

I glared at her. "Paranoid? Everyone in town should be paranoid. Those girls murdered Friday night should have been paranoid."

She ran a hand through her long red hair and sighed. "I assure you, Nikki, I had nothing to do with that."

I snorted. "Oh, well, if you say so."

We stared at each other for a few seconds and then she frowned. "What is your problem anyway?"

"You are my problem, you and your entire band of bloodthirsty monsters."

She threw her head back and laughed. "You're so melodramatic."

"Nikki, there isn't anyone up there," interrupted Nathan, as he walked back down the steps. "It was probably a bat or even an owl. We live near the woods, remember?"

I knew it was pointless arguing with him, so I went into the kitchen and grabbed a butcher knife.

"What in the hell are you going to do with that?" he asked as I hurried back into the great room.

"Protect myself, what else?"

He shook his head and turned to Celeste. "See what I mean?"

"Excuse me? What is that supposed to mean?" I snapped.

She licked her lips. "Oh, he was just telling me that ..."

"That you're delusional," smirked Nathan.

I scowled at him. "That's not funny."

"Jesus, I was just kidding. You're no fun at all these days," he sighed. "Listen, I'm going to throw in a pizza, would either of you like some?"

Both of us declined.

"Okay, suit yourselves. I'll be right back, Celeste. Make yourself at home," he said, heading towards the kitchen.

I turned to her. "What's wrong, don't enjoy your food cooked?"

She smiled. "Of course I do. I'm just not in the mood for... pizza."

The way she looked at me gave me the chills. I sat down in the club chair across the room and studied her, trying to decide what she wanted with my brother. With her long, red hair, perfect complexion, and soft curves, I could certainly understand why he was attracted to her, but what was she doing with him? What did she really want?

"So," I said, changing the subject. "If you weren't responsible for those girls the other night, who do you think was?"

She sighed and sat down on the leather sectional. "Truthfully, I don't really know."

I raised my eyebrows. "What, there's a rogue vampire in your midst?"

She shrugged and then studied her nails, which were long and painted blood-red.

Go figure.

"Great, a crazy rogue vampire," I huffed.

She rolled her eyes. "Vampire, such a droll term for us; we prefer to be called 'Roamers' or even 'Travelers.'"

I raised my eyebrows. "Travelers? Does that mean you'll be leaving soon?"

"Mm... yeah, probably. We don't like to stay in one place for too long."

Thank God.

"Why are you leaving this time, to avoid suspicion?"

She smiled wickedly. "Let's just say my brethren get bored with their menus very easily."

I shuddered. "That sounds so cold and heartless. We aren't animals."

"Sorry, it's just the way it is. The guys like a little variety and when things get stagnant, they just want to pick up and leave. I'm just along for the ride. I couldn't care less if we stayed or left. Food doesn't taste any different here than it does in another state."

"You're nothing but coldblooded murderers," I said, gripping the arms of the chair. I couldn't believe how impassive she was when talking about murder.

"Call us what you want. Just like you, we eat to live. It's not our fault that humans possess the nutrients we need to survive. Like I told you once before, survival of the fittest."

"But it's insane! How about getting blood from a blood bank or something? Or farming your own animals?"

She grinned. "Why do all the work in farming when our preferred animals can raise and feed themselves?"

I stood up and raised my knife, pointing it towards her. "Okay, what the hell do you really want with my brother?"

Celeste smiled at the way my hand shook, wielding the weapon. "I like him. He's cute, funny, and has a wonderful...scent."

I was now in such a rage that I could barely speak. "Get the hell out of my house," I demanded.

"Oh, hell, I'm just giving you shit," she giggled, clapping her hands. "Holy, shit, you should see your face!"

I stared at her incredulously. "Oh, you seriously think this is funny?"

"A little," she answered, brushing away a piece of lint from her short, black skirt. "Listen, your family has nothing to fear from me or my father. The other boys, well, I can't really speak for them. But I like Nathan and my father obviously adores your mother, so just chill out, Nikki."

"I'm sorry, but I don't trust you, Caleb, or any of your so-called 'Roamers.' Obviously, one of them is responsible for killing those girls."

"No, I don't think so. In fact, I have my own suspicions."

"What would that be?"

She leaned forward and murmured. "It's possible that Ethan is back."

That threw me off guard. I stared at her in shock.

"Did you hear me?" she asked.

"You think it was Ethan?" I whispered, touching my throat.

Celeste smiled. "Ah...so that excites you."

I scowled. "I'm not *excited* about Ethan in the least. He almost killed me before he left."

She waved her hand. "Oh, if Ethan wanted to kill you, he would have."

The possibility that Ethan had returned to Shore Lake stirred up emotions I didn't want to visit – ever again. I swallowed. "So, um why do you think Ethan might be involved?"

She looked at me like I was an idiot. "Revenge, of course. I mean, Caleb shot him. He's probably pissed as all hell and trying to create problems for my father now."

"But to kill those girls just to get back at your dad? Ethan told me he wasn't a murderer."

She looked at me incredulously. "And you trust him? I thought you didn't trust any Roamers?"

I ignored her question. "You know him better than I do. Would he lie to me?" I asked warily.

She raised an eyebrow. "You're really asking me?"

I sighed. "I don't really know who or what to believe anymore."

She stood up and walked over to the fireplace mantle. She picked up a photo of my brother and me. "If I were you," she said, putting the photo back and turning to me. "I wouldn't trust anyone, either; especially Ethan."

Chapter Four

Celeste left right after Nathan brought out the pizza.

"Are you sure you can't stay? I won't be able to eat all of this by myself," he said, trying to give her one of his puppy-dog looks.

He was so pathetic.

"It's getting too late," she said, grabbing her coat.

"Yeah, won't daddy be worried about you?" I asked sarcastically.

She smiled. "Well, he certainly knows I can handle myself. Plus, I promised him I'd bring back a late night snack on the way home."

I opened my mouth to say something, but from the look on her face, I knew she'd said it to get me fired up again. I decided to let it go.

"Okay," said Nathan, licking pizza from his fingers. He walked over to her and gave her a friendly hug. "I wish you'd let me drive you home."

"I'll be fine," she said, flashing him one of her blindingly white smiles.

"Okay, but I still feel funny about this. If anything happened to you, I'd never forgive myself."

She twirled a strand of her hair around her finger and batted her eyelashes. "Oh, Nathan, you're so sweet."

I wanted to throw up. The monster was flirting with my brother like she was a typical teenaged girl. I truly hated her just as much as my brother was truly smitten.

"Maybe we can hang out again next weekend?" he asked.

She pushed her hair behind her ears and nodded. "Yeah. I was thinking about checking out that new club, Nightshade."

"Don't you have to be twenty-one to get in?" I asked.

She smiled. "Yeah, but I can get you in. I know how to bribe the bouncers. In fact, I know a couple of them."

I'll bet.

"That sounds awesome," smiled Nathan.

"You should come, too," said Celeste, turning back towards me. "I'm sure it will be a blast."

"I have plans," I answered, quickly.

"Right," said Nathan. "You're coming, too, Twerp. You need to get out more. You're turning into a paranoid old lady and you're not even out of high school. Plus, I'm sure Duncan will be tagging along."

I snorted. "I doubt Duncan will go if he finds out I'm going."

"I doubt that," said Celeste, opening the front door. "I think Duncan has a thing for you."

"Maybe once, but not anymore," I muttered as Nathan walked her outside. He probably hated me and I didn't blame him one bit.

***

We didn't see our mother until almost nine o'clock Sunday night. She was paler than ever and looked so thin, her clothing practically hung off of her.

"Mom," scowled Nathan as she removed her long, brown coat. "You don't look well. Isn't that sheriff feeding you?"

She removed her sunglasses and laughed. "He's actually a wonderful cook. I just haven't been very hungry lately."

"Jeez, I wonder why..." I mumbled.

"What was that, Nikki?" she asked.

I cleared my throat. "Nothing. How are your eyes doing?" I answered.

She sighed. "Still very sensitive."

Nathan shook his head as she walked by him towards the steps. "Mom, you're skin and bones. I'm making you a sandwich," said Nathan. "Maybe two."

She yawned. "I'm really not hungry. I just need a shower and some rest."

He folded his arms across his chest. "Well then take some vitamins or something. You're scaring me."

She smiled. "Thanks for your concern, 'dad', but I'm fine."

I stared at her and thought about how much she'd changed over the last couple of months. Not all of it had been bad, in fact, I'd never seen her so happy in my life. It was her health that I was worried about; that and the fact that she was only a few steps away from being one of those Roamers.

After she went upstairs, Nathan turned to me. "I'm really worried about her. First the eye thing and now she's skin and bones. Maybe she has some kind of virus or something?"

I sighed. "You're so blind."

"What the hell is that supposed to mean?" he asked gruffly.

I leaned forward. "She's been bitten by a vampire. I can't believe you don't remember any of this stuff."

He looked at me with disgust. "Don't start this again."

I brushed him away and went upstairs to my room. His ignorance was so frustrating and it was clear whose side he was on.

Celeste's.

Because it looked like I was on my own with everything, I decided to do some more research on vampires. As I grabbed the book from the den and began reading it, there was a soft knock on my door.

"Nikki?" murmured my mother.

"Yes?"

She walked in, sat down at the edge of my bed and cleared her throat. "I wanted to let you know that Caleb and I are going out of town next weekend."

A cold fist wrapped around my heart and began squeezing; I could barely breathe. "What?"

She smiled. "We're going to Vegas."

"Vegas?"

Her eyes began to sparkle. "Yes, and I'm so excited. I've always wanted to go!"

"You can't," I whispered hoarsely.

Her face fell. "What do you mean?"

I swallowed the lump in my throat. "Mom, you can't go away with him. He's…"

She frowned. "He's what?"

I knew she'd be pissed but I had to fight for her and the rest of my family. I didn't want Caleb turning her into a full-fledged vampire. "He's a vampire."

She groaned. "We've been through this before. You know, I think Nathan is right; you need to talk to someone about this paranoia of yours. It's not healthy."

"Mom –" I argued.

"No," she shook her head. "This is getting to be way out of hand. I'm going to make an appointment for you sometime this week. I mean really, Nikki, a vampire? Caleb?"

"Well," I pointed towards her neck, which I noticed was covered. "How do you explain those marks on your neck?"

"What marks?" she asked, pulling her green turtleneck away from her skin. "You mean these hickies?"

I stared at her neck in horror. There were indeed red circular marks on her skin, but they weren't from bites. "Hickies? What are you guys, sixteen? Come on, mom, I'm talking about the bites from last summer. Remember those?"

"Yes," she nodded. "And I told you before, they were just some kind of allergic reaction, the insect bites are long gone now."

"Mom," I begged. "You have to believe me! Ethan was a vampire, Celeste is a vampire, and Caleb is definitely a vampire."

She shook her head sadly. "This whole thing with your father has really taken a toll on you. I think the sooner we schedule a meeting with a counselor or therapist, the better."

Before I could respond again, she kissed the top of my head and left the room.

This is insane, I thought. *How in the world was I going to stop my mom from going to Vegas?*

Feeling helpless and frustrated, I lay my head back on my pillow and closed my eyes, wondering what the hell I was going to do next. Within minutes I was fast asleep with the disturbing images of vampires, again, haunting my dreams.

Chapter Five

Sometime after eleven-thirty, my cell phone began to vibrate, startling me awake. When I recognized the number, I answered it immediately.

I cleared my throat. "Duncan?"

"We need to talk," he murmured.

The sound of his voice stirred up some of the butterflies that had been dormant for the last couple of months. Although my hands were shaking slightly, I tried to remain impassive on the phone. "Um, sure, how about tomorrow night, after work?"

"Actually, I'm right outside; can you meet me by the garage?"

I smiled. "Sure, can you just give me a few minutes?"

"Yeah."

I hung up and slipped on a pair of jeans, a light brown sweater, and my short leather boots. Because it was the end of October and the nights were getting frosty, I also grabbed a short gray wool jacket. Thankfully, Nathan and my mother were both sleeping, so I didn't have to explain myself as I slipped out the front door and into the cool darkness.

"Over here," called Duncan, as I stepped off of the porch. He was leaning against his white work truck, his hands in the front pockets of his faded jeans. Remembering the times we'd spent alone in his truck, I felt something tug at my heartstrings. Smiling hesitantly, I walked over to him.

"It's chilly," he murmured, looking up into the night sky. "Let's talk in the cab."

I nodded and went around to the passenger side and got in.

Starting it up, he turned on the heat and rubbed his hands. "Man, I forgot how cold it gets this time of year."

Delighted that he was even talking to me, I didn't trust myself to say anything that might ruin the moment. I just nodded and waited for him to tell me what was on his mind.

Staring ahead, he brushed a hand through his dark hair and sighed. "So, I think someone's stalking me."

My eyes widened. "Stalking you?"

Duncan turned to me, his silvery-gray eyes shining in the moonlight. "I noticed it a couple of weeks ago and it's just gotten worse. There have been shadows and strange noises just outside of my house."

The shadows didn't shock me in the least, especially with vampires prowling around town. "What kind of strange noises?"

He licked his lips. "Whispers. Eerie voices in the darkness. And then, last night, I actually heard footsteps on my roof, right above my bedroom."

I leaned back against the seat and folded my arms under my chest. "Well, it's obvious, isn't it?"

He narrowed his eyes. "What do you mean?"

"Vampires," I said, staring out towards the dark woods, wondering if any were watching us at that precise moment. I really wasn't worried about myself, but Duncan. He didn't have any protection, not even from Caleb or Celeste. "Don't you remember anything that happened last summer either?"

His face darkened. "The things that I remember have nothing to do with vampires."

"Duncan, it had *everything* to do with vampires. The problem is that some of your memories have been erased."

He stared at me for a minute and the shook his head.

"It's the truth," I said.

"Well, whoever erased my memories sure had a cruel sense of humor because they left only the painful ones," he answered with a tight smile.

I reached out and grabbed his arm. I needed him to understand.

"Listen," I pleaded, "you have to believe me, Ethan is a vampire, I swear to you, he is a vampire and he has this...this... control over my mind. I just couldn't resist him. I wasn't trying to hurt you."

He shook my hand away. "Do you really expect me to believe that? That he somehow hypnotized you and made you do things? I saw you returning his kisses on the beach and you were definitely enjoying the hell out of them."

I didn't know what to say. Part of me wasn't even sure what had happened on that night. Ethan had always been so seductive and irresistible. "I..."

Just then something landed on the hood of the truck with a loud thud and I cried out in shock.

"Holy shit!" gasped Duncan.

Ethan.

"Oh, my God," I squeaked.

He stared at the both of us, a dark smile spreading across his handsomely familiar face.

"Speak of the devil," muttered Duncan. "Where in the fuck did he come from?"

Ethan jumped off the hood and swaggered towards the passenger door with purpose.

He was coming for me!

I was so frightened, I could barely breathe. "Leave," I managed to blurt out. "Go, get us out of here!"

"Already ahead of you," replied Duncan, slamming the truck into gear. Soon we were flying through the bumpy yard and towards the dirt road leading to the freeway.

"See," I yelled, turning to look back. "I told you! He came from out of the sky! He's a fucking vampire!"

Duncan didn't say anything; he just kept glancing through his rearview mirror as we sped away towards the main road.

Not seeing anything but darkness, I turned back to the front and gasped. A lone figure, who had to be Ethan, was about fifty yards ahead of us, standing directly in our path.

"Hold on," ordered Duncan, noticing it as well.

"Oh, my God!" I yelled, holding onto the dashboard as Duncan pulled hard to the right, trying to avoid hitting Ethan. Before I knew what was happening, something slammed into the side of the truck and we began to roll.

"Duncan!" I screamed, my body slamming into his. The last thing I remembered before the darkness swallowed me up was the sound of glass shattering and Duncan's groans.

Chapter Six

"Nikki."

My eyes fluttered open against the brightness of a strange hospital room. As my eyes adjusted to the light, I noticed an I.V. sticking out of my arm. The other was bandaged and sore.

"Good, you're awake."

I turned towards the sound of my mother's voice. I was still groggy and it took me a few seconds to respond. "Mom," I whispered.

She cleared her throat. "The doctor said you'll be fine, honey. You sprained your wrist, have a few bruised ribs, and a concussion, but other than that, we can take you home as soon as you feel up to it."

I licked my dry lips. "Duncan?"

She gave me a puzzled look. "What about Duncan?"

"We…we were in his truck. It flipped…"

She shook her head in confusion. "No. Nathan found you near the bottom of that large oak tree just outside of your bedroom window. He thought you might have tried climbing it and fell or something."

My eyes widened in shock. "What?"

"Yes. Early this morning, he heard some kind of loud noise and found you unconscious, just lying there. Thank God Nathan found you when he did. You could have gotten hypothermia or something. It was pretty cold last night."

I shook my head. "No…no… no… Duncan stopped by late last night. We were talking in his truck and then…Ethan…"

She raised her eyebrows. "Ethan?"

I nodded. "He was there, mom. First he jumped on Duncan's truck, and then tried blocking our path. We tipped over…and that's the last thing I remember."

Her cell phone began to ring. She looked at the caller I.D.

"Oh, it's Nathan," she murmured and then answered. I heard her relaying everything I'd told her and then she stared at me with deep worry lines etched across her forehead while he responded. "Okay," she murmured into the phone. "I'll let her know. We'll be home soon."

"What did he say?" I asked the moment she hung up.

She touched my hand, softly. "Um...Duncan's... missing. I guess Sonny hasn't seen him since Sunday afternoon. He didn't show up for work this morning, either."

"Oh, my God," I whispered in horror.

"I guess Sonny is really concerned about him."

"Mom," I said, trying to sit up. "Ethan must have done something to him. In fact, Duncan said someone was stalking him. That's why he stopped over. He wanted to talk to me about it."

She closed her eyes and put a hand to her forehead.

"Mom?"

She opened her eyes and I saw tears. "There's another possibility," she said. "I think your father may have found us."

Chapter Seven

I stared at my mother with alarm. "What do you mean?"

She walked over to the window and looked outside. "Someone's been following me, too. I've noticed a dark SUV tailing me a few times and yesterday, I could have sworn someone followed me through the mall." She wrapped her arms around herself. "I just have this feeling it's Galen."

My father, Galen, went A.W.O.L. after attacking my mother back in June. Although they'd been separated for over two years prior, he'd flipped out when she'd finally started dating other men, leaving her mentally and physically abused. He was the whole reason we'd left California for

Montana. She was terrified he'd hurt her again, especially after pressing charges.

"Well, how do you think he found us?"

She turned around and sighed. "Honey, he's a cop. I'm sure he has friends who could have helped."

I wasn't personally afraid of my father, he'd never hurt me or my brother in the past, but now I was terrified for her. "Does Nathan know?"

"I told him this morning. He's quite upset, obviously."

"What about Caleb? Did you tell him?"

She nodded. "Yes, he knows."

I felt a cold chill run up my spine. Although I was worried about my father getting his hands on my mom, I was also nervous about Caleb. What would he do to my dad? Was Caleb a murderer? I didn't want my dad killed, just stopped and put away.

"Mom," I said. "Let's go home."

***

Nathan was still working at the marina when we arrived back at the cabin sometime after six. On our way home I hadn't seen any sign of Duncan's truck at the side of the road, either, which was very odd, because I distinctively remembered the accident.

"That tree right there," pointed my mom. "You were lying there, unconscious."

I stared at it in confusion. Things weren't making sense, and for the first time since we'd moved, I wanted to talk to Caleb.

"Mom," I asked. "Is Caleb stopping by later tonight?"

"Not that I know of," she said.

"Well, I'd like to talk to him," I said.

She raised her eyebrows. "I could call him."

I nodded. "Yeah, if you could."

"Sure. Are you hungry? I can make you something to eat."

I went over to the sectional and sunk down. My wrist was sore and so was my head. "Yeah, that'd be great, thanks."

"Okay. Don't forget to let Rosie know you won't be in this week."

"That's right," I said, reaching for my cell phone.

First I called Duncan's phone but it went to voicemail, then I called the diner to let them know what had happened.

"Well, I'm glad you're okay, honey," said Rosie. "You just take it easy now and when you're ready to come back, you give me a call."

"Rosie," I asked, "you haven't seen Ethan or any of his friends around lately, have you?"

"No, it's been a couple of months since I've seen those boys. But there was a young man in last night asking about you."

I raised my eyebrows. "A young man? Really?"

"Yes, about your age, really nice looking, too. I've never seen him before. I figured it was someone from school. He just asked if you were working and I told him you'd be in tonight. Obviously, you won't."

"I doubt it's someone from school," I murmured, wondering what that was all about.

"Well, he may come around again and I'll try and get more information. By the way, you haven't seen Duncan around, have you?" she asked. "Sonny stopped by earlier, just frantic with worry. I guess he's missing now."

I sighed. "No, I haven't, not since last night."

She sighed. "Dear God, I hope nothing happened to him, he's such a nice boy. First, those girls were murdered Friday night, and now he's missing. There are some strange things going on in this town."

Thinking about the possibility of Duncan, who was so good and kind, being murdered made my eyes fill with tears. "There sure is."

"Well, listen," she said. "I've got to get going. Take care of yourself, and like I said, when you're ready to come back, just call me."

I brushed a stray tear from my cheek. "Thanks, Rosie."

I hung up with her and went into the kitchen where my mother was currently fixing me a tuna fish sandwich. I sat down at the counter and watched her, wondering if she'd even eaten lately. She was thinner than ever.

"I spoke to Caleb," she said, smiling brightly. "He said he'll swing by around ten tonight."

I nodded. "Thanks."

She leaned forward and brushed a strand of hair from my eyes. "Don't worry, honey," she said softly. "They'll find Duncan. I know how much you care about him."

As far as finding him went, I wasn't so sure about that, but I also knew that Caleb was the only one who might have answers. I forced a smile. "I hope so."

She went to the fridge, grabbed the milk, and poured us each a glass. Then she slid one over to me and sat down. "Just don't give up hope. That's what you've always told me."

I stared at my sandwich and nodded. "Speaking of which, what are you going to do about dad?"

She looked at her milk and grimaced. "I don't know. I'm not even positive that he or anyone else is really following me. Maybe it's my imagination?"

"Maybe it's Ethan. I told you he was here last night."

She pushed her untouched glass of milk away. "That's what Caleb mentioned when I filled him in on what was happening. In fact, he doesn't want either of us leaving the cabin until he gets over here tonight."

"Mom," I said, staring at her thin, bony cheeks. "When was the last time you ate?"

"I had some eggs for breakfast. I've just been kind of nauseated lately. Maybe I'm pregnant," she said with a teasing smile.

I groaned. "No, don't even say that. That's cruel."

Her eyes twinkled. "Oh, it wouldn't be so bad, would it? The pitter patter of little feet, toys strung out everywhere. Reruns of Barney playing, over and over..."

Bottles of blood, warming in the microwave...

I shivered. "Don't even go there. Aren't you, like, a little ancient to be having babies now anyway?"

Her jaw dropped. "I'm not that old. Women are having babies in their forties all the time. I'm not *even* forty."

"Well, whatever the case may be, you need to eat. You don't look healthy at all."

"I'm fine, just worry about yourself and keeping that wrist straight," she said, looking at my bandage.

I moved my wrist slightly and winced, it was pretty tender. "I will."

She stood up. "Listen, I'm going to take a shower and read for a while before Caleb gets here. Nathan should be home pretty soon."

I nodded and watched her leave. I was going to have a talk with Caleb about her, as well. She was obviously starving to death and I knew it had to be something related to whatever he'd done to her. My only consolation was that she didn't appear to be a vampire yet.

After I was done eating, I went upstairs with my cell phone, to try and reach Duncan again. I was terrified that Ethan had killed him, and I felt more than a little responsible. As expected, Duncan didn't answer.

Sighing, I checked the time and noticed it was after eight, so I decided to take a shower and then wait for Caleb, too. I carefully removed the bandage before getting in and it was a total pain in the ass, taking me almost forty-five minutes to finish my shower. When I was finally done, I wrapped my wrist back up, slipped on a pair of sweats and a T-shirt, then stepped back into my bedroom.

"What the hell?" I hollered.

She looked up. "Oh, hi."

Celeste was lounging on the bed, painting her perfect nails with *my* new copper nail polish.

"How did you get in here?" I snapped.

She smiled. "You left your balcony door unlocked. That's very dangerous, you know. There are things out there...." She shuddered.

I crossed my arms under my chest and glared at her. I was still irritated that she was making herself at home. "So, what... you fly, too?"

"Not very often," she answered, blowing on her tips. "Tonight, I drove. Flying is a killer on the hair."

The image of someone like her flying through the darkness was almost comical. Tonight, she was definitely dressed to party in a shimmery silver dress and dark stiletto heels. Her fiery red hair was piled high above her narrow shoulders and she wore silver cross earrings on her lobes.

"Don't those earrings bother you?" I asked incredulously.

She touched her ears, then threw her head back and laughed so hard, I saw a hint of fang. "Why, because they're 'cross' earrings?"

"Well, yeah."

She waved her hand at me. "No, not at all. I like garlic, too, by the way. And don't get me started on holy water. I'd bathe in it if I had to; wouldn't bother my skin one bit."

Obviously, my knowledge of true vampires was crap. I'd already learned that they could survive in the sun. Because of their extremely sensitive eyes, they just preferred... not to.

I sat down across from her on an oversized lime and pink beanbag chair. "So, did you hear about Duncan?" I asked, gauging her reaction.

Her eyes softened. "My dad told me about it. It's tragic."

"Tragic?" I looked at her in horror. "It's a nightmare. Ethan showed up last night, I ended up in the hospital, and Duncan is missing," I grumbled. "Tragic is even an understatement."

"I'm sorry for your loss," she answered. "Obviously, if Ethan got his hands on him and he's missing, he's... dead."

"What if he isn't dead? You have to help me find him," I begged, hating myself for having to do it.

She sighed and stood up. "I'll do what I can – because we're almost family now. Plus, I really like Duncan. He's a cutie."

Cringing, I ignored the "family" comment. "Have you or any of the others seen Ethan around?" I asked.

She turned to me. "No, but Ethan will be found only if he wants to be found."

Just then, my mom knocked on the door and opened it. "Nikki, Caleb's here already. Oh, hi, Celeste," she said, smiling. "I didn't know you were in here."

"I decided to drop by to see if I could help in any way."

My mom walked over and gave her a hug. "Oh, you're such a sweetheart."

As sweet as a ghost pepper, I thought.

We followed my mother downstairs, where Caleb was lounging in the great room. As soon as he saw us, he stood up and gave us one of his electric smiles.

"Good, you made it, Celeste," he said, stepping towards her. He hugged her close and I caught him whispering something into her ear.

She nodded.

"Anne, sweetheart," asked Caleb, after releasing his daughter. "Do you have any coffee? I'm simply wiped out."

My mother smiled at him adoringly. "Of course, I'll fix you a cup. Black, right?"

"Yes. Thanks, hon."

She nodded. "Anyone else?" she asked.

Celeste and I both shook our heads.

After my mom went into the kitchen, Celeste quickly headed for the door.

"You're leaving already?" I asked.

"She's going to make sure we're not being watched," interrupted Caleb. "I sensed another presence when I arrived."

I looked towards the windows, which were covered with blinds, and my stomach clenched. "Oh," I said.

"Don't worry; it's probably nothing, maybe a deer or bear. Now, sit down," said Caleb, motioning towards one of the club chairs, "and tell me what happened, last night."

I sank down into it. "Um, okay."

He moved across from me and leaned against the arm of the other chair while I gave him a rundown of the last twenty-four hours. I watched as his face darkened when I mentioned Ethan.

"He's lucky to be alive," he growled, standing up. He began to pace. "I let him live and now he dares to disobey me? This won't do."

The last time I'd seen Caleb this angry was when he'd caught Ethan trying to seduce me. That was the night he'd banished Ethan from Shore Lake. The last time I'd actually even spoken to Ethan.

I swallowed. "So, do you think he killed Duncan?"

Caleb turned to me, his eyes glowing slightly. "Probably, he's always been a loose cannon. Never liked to follow the rules much, either. After meeting you, he became even more unruly."

Normally Caleb didn't frighten me, but the way he was looking at me now was a little unnerving. There was a definite hunger fueled by rage that I saw reflected in his eyes, and something told me he was trying to restrain himself.

I stood up and moved farther away as nonchalantly as I could. "So, do you think he murdered those girls, too?"

I watched as his eyes began to glow even brighter. I guess talking about dead girls fired him up.

He licked his lips and nodded. "Possibly. I think it was definitely a Roamer. There was blood missing from the girls."

"What about the others in your group? Maybe they killed them and not Ethan?"

When he smiled this time, I could see his sharp fangs. "Oh...I know where this is going," he said, leaning forward. "The thought of him feeding on humans scares you."

"Well, yeah!" I said. "And to be honest, you're kind of scaring me right now, the way you're looking at me – like you're ready to pounce or something. Caleb, I seriously doubt my mom would be too happy if something happened to me and you were the only person around."

He closed his eyes for a few seconds, and when he opened them back up, I noticed a change. "Sorry," he smiled. "I haven't fed for a while. Sometimes the hunger is so strong, it takes control."

"Great," I muttered. "Maybe you should feed before you come to visit from now on."

"Don't worry," he said. "You're safe with me. I can control it."

From the way he had been looking at me before, I wasn't so sure.

"What about my mother?" I asked.

"What about your mother?"

"She's starting to look like a holocaust victim."

He frowned. "It's the cancer. I told you before. It's ravaging her body."

I raised my eyebrows. "Are you sure it's not from being bitten by you?"

He licked his lips and smiled. "I don't think you know what you're talking about."

"You told me..."

Just then, we heard screams of terror coming from the kitchen, and Caleb disappeared through the doors with lightning speed.

I jumped up to follow him when the front door crashed open. As I turned to look, something grabbed me and I was whisked outside into the darkness.

Chapter Eight

I struggled with my captor as we sped through the darkness, but he tightened his hold until I could do nothing but await my fate. When we finally stopped, we were in some kind of cold, abandoned factory. The moment we landed, his mouth began ravaging my flesh.

"Ethan," I gasped, trying to dislodge myself from his embrace.

"Oh, God I've missed you," he groaned, his lips trailing a wave of heat all along my neckline.

With all my might, I shoved him away. "Please," I breathed, as his icy blue eyes locked with mine. The raw hunger reflected there terrified me and I took a step back.

He glanced down at my bandaged wrist and scowled. "What happened to your arm, are you okay?"

I stared at him incredulously. "Okay? Am I okay? You just kidnapped me and the last time we were together... actually, the last two times... you almost killed me."

Ethan stepped towards me and gripped my shoulders. "No. That's not true," he murmured. "I'd never harm you, not intentionally."

"You drained me of too much blood, Ethan. And then last night..."

He raised his eyebrows. "Last night?"

I glared at him. "Yeah, last night! You showed up and scared the shit out of me and Duncan! The truck rolled, I ended up in the hospital and Duncan... where is he, by the way? What have you done with him?"

"I don't know what you're talking about," he answered with a totally perplexed look. "I just got back into Shore Lake tonight."

"That's bull crap!" I hollered, hitting him with my good arm. "I saw you last night. Don't lie to me!"

"I swear I wasn't here. In fact, I've been with Drake in New York and it wasn't until tonight that Julian found me and told me what was happening. I rushed back here to make sure you were okay."

I stared at him, wondering if he was insane. The person staring at me last night was definitely

Ethan. Unless he had a twin – a vampire twin – there was no mistaking his handsome face. He had to have been lying.

"You're not going to tell me what you did to Duncan, are you?" I whispered in horror.

"I haven't seen that guy since the night I left." He ran a hand through his dark hair. "Obviously something is going on around here and I'm being framed for it."

I snorted. "Now, why would someone do that? And how would it even be possible?"

He smiled bitterly. "I've made a lot of enemies, Nikki," he said. "And some of those beings have incredible powers, well beyond even my capabilities. You can't even imagine the things they can do."

"Are you saying there are more dangerous things out there than you Roamers?" I asked incredulously.

He threw his head back and laughed. "Roamers? That's a riot. I see you've been talking to Celeste."

I crossed my arms under my chest and frowned. "Well, you're certainly not human. I mean, you drink blood and can obviously fly like the wind."

"I may not be human... anymore, but we have the same feelings, Nikki, and urges..." he answered with a seductive tilt of his lips. "Ours are just more intense."

I felt my face turn red and attempted to change the subject. "So, um... you think you were framed? Well, what are you going to do now?"

With a determined look in his eyes, he moved towards me, and soon I was back in his arms and something inside of me began to stir.

I cursed myself. *Why couldn't I resist him?*

"What am I going to do now?" he whispered into my hair. "Well, I'm glad you asked..."

"Please, just bring me home, this isn't right," I pleaded, closing my eyes, breathing in his sweet butterscotch scent.

For the love of God, how could anyone resist him?

"Right? It's totally right." He inhaled deeply, "God, you smell wonderful."

Since he was both man and vampire, I wasn't sure if smelling wonderful to him was a good or bad thing. Before I could consider the consequences of smelling good, he raised my chin and captured my mouth with his. When his tongue pushed through my lips and sought mine, I gave in and pulled him closer, taking in his heat.

I opened my eyes.

Heat?

It was obvious that he'd recently fed.

Fed on Duncan?

"You've fed?" I choked, pushing him away.

He shrugged. "It's been a while, but I'm in complete control. Don't worry," he said. "I just need to feel you. That's all I want."

He grabbed me again and just like before, I surrendered and forgot about everything else. I melted into his arms, returning his kisses freely. Soon, his mouth moved down to my neck and his hands were under my sweatshirt, exploring my breasts. When he pushed my bra away and lowered his mouth to my nipples, I shuddered in pleasure.

"So beautiful," he whispered, licking my flesh, sending shivers all the way down to my toes. "My sweet little ...Nikki..."

"Yes," I breathed, wanting to be his forever.

His mouth was magical, making me forget about everything but the moment. I slid my hand into his soft hair and drew him closer to my breasts. "Ethan," I whimpered as the fire he'd ignited grew hotter between my thighs. Soon I was trembling, my body aching for something that both frightened and excited me.

"Say my name, again..." he growled, his voice husky with desire.

I threw my head back and moaned as his mouth ravaged my flesh, making me delirious with need; a need so strong I was willing to do anything for him at that moment. "Oh...God...Ethan..."

He sucked in a breath. "Nikki, God...I'm inhaling your excitement and it's driving me insane. I want you so bad but...God... we can't do this here," he said, abruptly removing his hands from my skin. "You deserve much better than this."

"Wait," I reached out, not wanting him to stop. His touch created a primal need like nothing I'd never known before. I had to have more of him and didn't want to wait for anything. "I don't mind. Really, it's okay," I whispered.

"No, it's not," he said, looking around in disgust. "It's cold and dirty here. When this happens between us, and believe me, Nikki," he smiled darkly, "it will, I want it to be in a place that's comfortable, clean, and safe. Not a shithole like this."

My heart pounded in my chest as I stared at him. He was so sexy, so amazingly beautiful, and his eyes...oh...his eyes...they held an inhuman fire that probably should have frightened me, but instead, made me only want him more. "Why can't I resist you?" I whispered.

"Because, we belong together," he replied, kissing the tip of my nose. He then pulled me to his chest and whispered, "Forever."

The way he said "forever" brought me back to reality. I wanted him, boy did I ever want him, but his "forever" was something much different than mine.

I cleared my throat. "I...I think I should go home," I said, avoiding his eyes as I pulled away.

"What's wrong?"

I stared at him in exasperation. "Everything is wrong, Ethan. I still don't know what happened to Duncan, and…"

It was then that I'd remembered my mother's terrified screams right before Ethan had snatched me from the cabin. "My mother," I said, staring at him in horror. "Did you frighten her? She was screaming when we left."

He looked hurt. "No, Nikki, I wouldn't do that. Someone else scared your mom. In fact, a man was looking into the kitchen window. But don't worry, Celeste took care of him."

"A man?"

He nodded. "Yeah, in fact, he kind of looked like your brother."

I suddenly felt sick to my stomach.

Was it my father? He definitely looked like Nathan. More like an older brother than a father. Who else could it be?

"You have to get me home," I pleaded. "I think it's my dad and I have to make sure everyone's okay."

He sighed. "If that's what you want."

"It is. Please."

He picked me up and cradled me in his arms. "Hold on tight."

I slid my good hand around his neck and stared at his chiseled features in fascination. At that moment, I felt like some all-American superhero was carrying me off somewhere into the night, not a bloodthirsty vampire. It was a nice, whimsical fantasy. One that was also very dangerous.

Chapter Nine

When we arrived back at the cabin, the lights were out and the only vehicle around was mine.

"Look," said Ethan, pointing towards the windows near the kitchen. The floodlights were on, lighting up the yard. "Something happened here."

I walked over and looked down at the dirt. It definitely looked like some kind of scuffle had occurred.

Ethan bent down and touched the ground. "I smell blood," he murmured. "Looks like someone tried cleaning it up. But I definitely sense that it was human blood."

My eyes filled with tears. "I wonder if it was my dad and they killed him."

"Celeste attacked the man, whoever he was, without hesitation. She probably fed off of him when it was over and then hid the body."

I shuddered. "Are you sure? She doesn't seem that heartless."

His eyes narrowed. "Don't ever underestimate Celeste. She's dangerous. In fact, I've watched her tear people to shreds without a second thought. I think you should stay away from her from now on."

Thinking about my dad being murdered by anyone was unsettling. Even though he was an asshole, he was still my father and there were some good memories.

I brushed a couple of the tears from my cheeks. "She told me to trust her and Caleb. That neither of them would hurt us. You think she's lying?"

He shrugged. "I don't know. But to be safe, it's better if you stay as far away from her as possible."

Just then, we saw a pair of headlights moving towards us in the distance.

"Your brother," said Ethan. "I should leave."

"You can see that far?" I asked, incredulously.

He smiled and pulled me to him. "Go inside and wait for him. I'll check around town and see what's happening."

I nodded.

"Nikki," he said. "I swear to you, I didn't kill anyone, and I have no idea what happened to Duncan." His face darkened. "Someone is playing a dangerous game, and when I find out, I can't promise that there won't be any blood spilled. Nobody fucks with me."

I opened my mouth to say something, but he placed a finger over my lips to silence me.

"I love you," he continued, his eyes burning into mine. "You may not believe it and, to tell you the truth," he said, smiling. "I'm not even sure how it happened so fast. But, I love you and I'm coming back for you. Just give me a couple days to figure out what's happening."

"Okay," I whispered.

He then pressed his lips to mine and kissed me more tenderly than I thought possible. I closed my eyes and relished the way his mouth explored mine and how oddly wonderful he smelled. When he finally pulled away, I groaned in protest.

"Until we meet again," he said, backing away.

I raised my hand and waved just as my brother's headlights surrounded me.

"Who the fuck was that?!" yelled Nathan, slamming the door of his Mustang. "And what the hell is going on around here?"

I stared at him, not knowing exactly where to begin. "Truthfully," I said. "I don't know what's happening. And I doubt you'd even believe me if I told you."

"Mom called me and she's worried sick about you! She and Caleb are out scouring the town looking for your ass!"

I cleared my throat. "Well, I'm fine."

He laughed coldly. "I see that. Who was with you just now?" His eyes scanned the woods. "Did he just take off somewhere into the woods?"

"It doesn't matter, it's just a friend. Listen, Nathan, I think dad was here and that he might have been hurt."

He raised his eyebrows. "Dad?"

"Seriously."

Nathan ran a hand through his hair and looked around the yard. "Tonight?"

I nodded and then showed him the footprints near the kitchen window.

"This doesn't mean anything," he said, crouching down.

"Look," I said, pointing to some dark spots. "Blood."

He reached over and touched it. When his fingers came back up to the light, they were bloody. "Oh, shit," he whispered.

"Call mom," I said.

He nodded, then took out his cell phone and dialed her number. I listened as he explained that I was home now and how we'd discovered some blood right outside of the kitchen window.

"Oh," he said, nodding after listening to her response. "Okay. Well, I'll let her know. I guess she was with some friend or something," he said, looking at me with a frown. "Don't worry, I'll let her know."

"What?" I asked when he hung up.

"First of all, she said you're grounded because you took off and had everyone worried. Second of all, the blood was from a raccoon that tried attacking Celeste. Celeste killed it and Caleb helped to get rid of it."

I closed my eyes and groaned. It was like talking to a wall. He'd never believe me. "Where's mom now?"

"On her way home."

"Okay," I sighed, feeling mentally exhausted. I wasn't going to win any arguments tonight. "I'm going up to bed."

"Wait," said Nathan as I climbed the steps. "How's your wrist?"

I shrugged. "Pretty sore still. It's sprained."

He nodded. "Have you heard anything from Duncan yet?"

"No," I said. "The last time I saw him was yesterday when we were attacked."

He stepped closer to me. "Attacked?"

I frowned. "I know you don't believe me, but we were attacked and now he's missing. I mean, come on, Nathan, why would I be climbing a tree in the middle of the night?"

He stared at the tree in question. "I know. It didn't make much sense to me either. But then again, you've been acting very strange lately. Especially with all of your vampire ramblings."

"It's true," I said. I then told him about my conversations with Celeste and Caleb.

He gave me a pained expression. "Here we go again."

I groaned. "Why are you being so pig-headed?"

"You know why, Nikki! Vampires don't exist!"

I rubbed my forehead, I was getting another headache. "I'm going to bed. Obviously, you're not going to be any help finding Duncan."

He followed me up the steps to the porch. "Are you going to school tomorrow?"

"I'm going to try," I answered.

We walked into the house and I went upstairs to my room. When I finally shut my eyes and started drifting off, it was well past midnight.

Chapter Ten

Luckily, I managed to get up in time for school the next morning. After being lectured from my mother for ten minutes, I took a quick shower, slipped on a long plum sweater and jeans, then grabbed a Pop-Tart to eat on the way to school.

"Don't forget, you're grounded!" called my mom, who was also leaving for work.

I rolled my eyes and grabbed my car keys. "Right."

Like she would even be home to check on me, I thought. She was spending more time at Caleb's than at home.

School was as boring and uneventful as usual. Everyone asked me about my wrist and I gave them some lame excuse about falling out of a tree after trying to rescue a cat. It was better than the truth, which would have made me the laughing stock of school.

During lunch, I sat down with a couple of girls from history class and they started talking about Duncan. Apparently, they'd heard Sonny was starting a search party to look for him since he was still missing. I decided to join when school was out.

"I'm coming, too," said Nathan in the parking lot at the end of the day. "Sonny's closed the marina and needs all the help he can get."

"I'd better let mom know," I said, sending her a text. I seriously doubted she'd be mad about me skipping out of being grounded when it came to finding Duncan. Fortunately, I was right.

Be home at a reasonable hour, she texted back. *Good Luck.*

I met Nathan at the marina, where we met some volunteers who were organizing the different search teams. We ended up getting assigned to an area near our cabin, which was good because that's where he'd disappeared. As we were leaving, Sonny showed up, looking distraught.

"Any news?" asked Nathan.

He shook his head. He had bags under his eyes and his face was etched with worry lines. He seemed to have aged overnight. "No, nothing."

"We're going back towards our cabin to see if there are any clues or anything. Nikki claims she saw him there the night he disappeared."

Sonny raised his eyebrows and turned to me. "Really?"

I wanted to tell him everything, but from the distraught look in his eyes, I just couldn't add to his stress. For one, it wouldn't help matters, and for another, he'd probably think I was completely insane.

"Yeah," I said. "He left the cabin pretty late and that was the last time I saw him."

Nathan's eyebrows went up but he didn't say anything.

"Did he mention where he was going when he left your place?"

I bit the side of my lip. "I think he was heading home." I felt horrible for lying but I didn't know what else to say.

Sonny took out a cigarette. "I should probably have you speak to the sheriff. He said he'd be here sometime around six."

"Yeah, I'd actually like to talk to him, too," I said. Both Caleb *and* Celeste.

It was almost four by the time we left the marina. Nathan and I had actually decided to leave our vehicles at home and begin our own search, starting with the woods around our house. He grabbed a flashlight so we could continue our search even when the sun went down.

"Let me show you the spot where I think we flipped over in the truck," I said.

He was unusually quiet as we walked through the yard and towards the dirt road. It took us about ten minutes to reach the area where I thought the accident occurred.

"This is it," I said, pointing towards the tire marks on the side leading into the grass. "Look at those tire tracks."

"Yeah, and look over here," he said, motioning towards an area of grass that was flattened. "This must have been where it rolled. There's even some debris left over."

Sure enough, there were some broken pieces of glass and metal that had been forgotten by whoever had cleared the accident.

"So, do you believe me now?" I asked, picking up a piece of a broken taillight.

He turned to me, his face grim. "To be honest, I don't really know what to believe. Either I'm almost as nuts as you, or there's something very sinister going on here."

"Nathan," I said, standing up. "I need to tell you this...last night I was with Ethan."

His jaw clenched. "What the hell, Nikki? That guy's nothing but trouble. He's a deviant, and the last person in the world you should be associating with. What in the hell were you thinking?"

I raised my chin and glared at him. "Well, I didn't go with him on my own free will. He grabbed me and flew me to some abandoned building."

He shook his head and smirked. "Right, he flew you."

"Yeah, like I said, he's a vampire. If you don't start removing your head from your ass, you're going to find out the hard way that we are not alone out here. There are vampires or 'Roamers' as they prefer to be called."

"Roamers?"

I nodded. "Yes, Celeste is also a vampire, and she told me they prefer to be called Roamers or Travelers."

He started laughing. "You've got to be kidding."

I raised my sprained wrist. "Does this look like I'm kidding? Does the fact that Duncan is missing and more people are being murdered really sound like a joke to you?"

He raised his hands. "Okay, let's say that you're right, which I'm not saying you are, but hypothetically, if there are 'Roamers', which one of them is responsible for Duncan?"

I sighed. "That's the part I'm not really sure of. The night he went missing, I could have sworn it was Ethan who attacked us, but now, after talking to him, I'm not so sure."

He sighed. "Why not? Because he's a good kisser?"

Ethan was; I had to give him that.

"Because he said he was out of town and believes that someone is setting him up."

Nathan stared at me for a minute and then began laughing. "I...this is just too hard to accept. I was willing to try, but Jesus, Nikki."

I stepped towards him. "Just keep an open mind, please. That's all I ask."

Just then we both spotted Celeste's truck moving towards us. When she reached the spot where we were standing, she rolled down her window and smiled sweetly at Nathan. "Hey there, handsome! You weren't answering your phone so I thought I'd take a trip out here; I was just wondering if you were free tonight?"

"Well, I don't know, Celeste, we're kind of busy. You heard Duncan's missing, right?"

She tossed her red hair. "I heard, but I know he's just skipping town for a while."

I raised my eyebrows. "Oh, is that so?"

She nodded. "Yeah, he left me a message on my cell phone earlier today."

We both stared at her in shock. "You're kidding? Did you tell Sonny?"

She nodded. "I just got back from talking to him. I even had him listen to the voicemail, too."

"Sonny must be pissed," muttered Nathan. "Setting up this big search party and now finding out he just skipped out of town for a while."

"You could say he was a little pissed," she answered.

"What did he say?" I asked. I was hurt and confused. I'd left him several messages and he'd called *Celeste*?

"Duncan said he was confused about you," she said, staring at me with amusement. "That Ethan was still trying to come between you two and even went so far as to attack him the other night, just to get to you. He said he hit a tree and blacked out, when he woke up the next morning, you were gone and he assumed you'd left with Ethan, just like last time. He said it pissed him off so much that he drove to Minnesota where his mom lives. He needed time to think."

The story didn't make any sense at all. It didn't sound at all like Duncan, either. He wouldn't have left town that easily, especially without checking to make sure that I was okay. "We didn't hit a tree," I said. "We flipped, right here, as a matter of fact."

"Where's the truck then?" asked Nathan.

Great, now he was questioning me again. Like always.

I glared at him. "I don't know but we definitely flipped. I was there."

"So was Duncan," said Celeste. "Anyway, you can talk to him about it when he gets back."

I nodded. "Oh, I certainly will."

If he ever came back.

"So, what kind of plans did you have in mind for tonight?" smiled Nathan, all thoughts of Duncan replaced by his raging hormones.

She removed her sunglasses and gave him a sultry look. "I was thinking about checking out that new club. You in?"

"I thought you were waiting until Saturday?" I asked.

She nodded. "I was. But then my friend, Julian – he's a bouncer there – said they're having a private party tonight and I should invite some friends. Julian says this party is going to be off the charts!"

"You're just lucky you graduated last year, Celeste," said Nathan. "We aren't allowed to go clubbing on a school night."

She gave him a pouty look. "Oh, come on. Your mom's probably staying at my dad's tonight, anyway; she won't even know."

He sighed. "Nikki's grounded and I have to work tomorrow night. I'd be wiped out by then."

Something changed in her expression and I watched as Nathan's eyes seemed to dilate as he stared at her in wonder.

"Meet me there at ten o'clock," she murmured, running her nails over the hand he'd planted near her window. "I promise you won't regret it, Nathan."

"I wouldn't miss it," he answered, his eyes his face flushed.

"What the hell, Celeste?" I snapped.

She looked at me wide-eyed. "You're free to tag along." She smiled, giving me a hint of fang. "I won't bite."

I was so angry that I wanted to punch her, but I knew she'd kill me, literally. Instead, I just gave her a murderous look. "No, we're both skipping tonight's club invite. Sorry."

Nathan turned to me. "That's rude, Nikki. You don't have to come if you don't want to, but don't be such a bitch to Celeste!"

"You've got to be kidding me," I mumbled, shaking my head.

"Don't worry, Celeste," he said turning back to her. "I'll be there."

She gave me a triumphant smirk and then restarted the engine. Batting her eyes at my clueless brother, she said, "See you later, Nathan." Then she took off, kicking up rocks and dust in her wake.

"What was that all about?" he asked, turning back to me. "You don't have to be so damn rude to her all the time."

I shook my head. "She just put you in some kind of trance. Don't you even realize that?"

He scowled. "You're completely nuts."

I grabbed his arm. "Don't go out tonight. Mom will kill you if she finds out, Nathan."

He didn't answer me, just shook my hand away and started walking back towards the cabin.

Chapter Eleven

Feeling frustrated, I went to my bedroom to sulk and decided to remove the bandage from my wrist. It was still a little sore but the pressure from the bandage was bugging me and my skin was getting itchy. Once it was off, it felt so much better that I decided to call Rosie the following day to find out when I could come back. The idea of sitting at home grounded was too depressing anyway.

Grabbing some lotion with aloe to soothe my itchy arm, I went back downstairs to watch television and to find out if there were any more missing teens in town. Fortunately, the biggest story was about a sixty-year-old woman who'd just given birth to triplets. I thought about my mother giving birth to Caleb's child and shuddered, wondering if vampires could even impregnate people. I hoped to never find out the answer.

It was starting to get late and I sent my mom a text, wondering when she'd be coming home. Sure enough, she called me back right away and explained that she was going to stay at Caleb's again.

"Don't you have to work tomorrow?" I whined.

She cleared her throat. "Yeah, but I'm taking the morning off to do some shopping for the trip. I'm going out of town, remember?"

"How can I forget? God, mom, you're never home anymore," I complained. "And this weekend, you'll be in Vegas? We never see you anymore."

"Stop being so dramatic, Nikki. Jesus, why can't you just be happy for me?" she asked. "I've met a man who makes me happy and you two will be leaving for college soon. You know how I hate being alone," she murmured.

Yeah, well… so do we, I thought.

"What about your eyes?" I asked. "Won't all the bright lights in Vegas bother your irises or whatever's bothering you?"

She chuckled. "We'll be sleeping during the day and enjoying the city at night, like everyone else does. Anyway, I doubt we'll even be outdoors much. With all the shows and things that Caleb has planned for us."

I rolled my eyes. "Of course."

"Listen," she said, "tomorrow I'll take you and Nathan out to dinner to make it up to you. Somewhere nice, I promise."

"Whatever," I mumbled.

She groaned. "Nikki, just give me a break. It's only one weekend. Do you know how long it's been since I've been on vacation?"

It wasn't just one weekend that I was worried about. I somehow sensed that Caleb would be turning her into a vampire during their trip to Vegas, which would last a lifetime. He was going to take my mother away from me and it was tearing me apart. Just thinking about it, I began to panic.

"Mom," I begged. "Please don't go away this weekend. I'm... I'm...scared that something's going to happen to you."

She sighed. "Oh, you're being ridiculous. Look, I've got to go. We'll talk more about this tomorrow night."

"But..."

"Like I said, we'll talk about it tomorrow night. I love you, Nikki."

Before I could answer, she hung up the phone.

I sighed and tossed my phone off of the bed. It was after nine and I'd also had no luck talking Nathan out of going to Club Nightshade. I felt so powerless and frustrated. Part of me wanted to go to the club with him, but another part of me wanted to see if Ethan would pay me a visit. I was curious to see if he'd found out what the hell was going on.

"I'm leaving," declared Nathan, sticking his head into my doorway. "Last chance to tag along, Twerp."

I shook my head. "No way."

He sighed and then stepped into my bedroom. "Look," he said, sitting on the edge of my bed. "I know we've been arguing a lot lately, but I want you to know, I'm on your side."

I stared at my big-hearted brother with his deep dimples and bright blue eyes and was terrified that Celeste would harm him. I wanted to beg him to stay home, to tell him he was being manipulated, but I knew it would go in one ear and out the other. "Thanks," I answered. "Just be careful tonight."

He grinned. "If anyone should be careful, it's Celeste. When she gets a whiff of my new cologne, she's not going to be able to control herself."

"You're so pathetic," I said, unable to hide my smile.

He stood up and went over to my balcony door. "Keep this thing locked," he said, turning the knob. "If you really believe in boogiemen, then maybe you shouldn't be making it so easy for them to get into your bedroom."

I closed my eyes. "Goodbye, Nathan. Call me if you need me."

"You too," he said.

When he left, I opened my eyes and pulled out the butcher knife I'd hidden under my bed. If something bad was going to happen, at least I'd have a weapon.

***

I was sound asleep when something brushed against my arm, jerking me out of a deep sleep. I bolted upright and looked around the room, my heart beating wildly in my chest. When I was able to convince myself that I was really alone, I released a shaky breath and allowed myself to relax.

Wondering about the time, I looked at my alarm clock and breathed a sigh of relief. It was just past one and I still had five more hours of sleep before I had to worry about getting ready for school. I closed my eyes to try and fall back to sleep, when I noticed the chill in the air. My body began to shiver and I looked towards my balcony in horror; the door was wide open.

"Ethan?" I whispered, reaching for my knife.

Nobody answered.

I got out of bed and crept towards the balcony, terrified that someone was going to swoop in and kill me. When I finally reached the glass and peered outside, my jaw dropped.

"Duncan?"

He was sitting alone at the small bistro table on my balcony, staring out into the moonlight. He turned to me and cleared his throat. "Hey, Nikki."

I stepped outside and knelt next to him. "I'm so happy to see you," I said, my eyes welling with tears. I had no idea how much I'd missed him until now. "God, I thought you were dead."

He touched a strand of my hair. "I'm still here."

I swallowed the lump in my throat. "So, how long have you been sitting out here?"

He shrugged. "Not too long."

"Are you okay?" I asked, grabbing his hand. He was chilled to the bone.

He looked away. "I've been... better."

I rubbed his hand, trying to warm his skin. "You should really come inside. It's freezing out here."

He turned and stared at my hand as I continued to rub his. "Nikki, I really don't think that's a good idea."

"Why?" I teased. "Does being alone with me in my bedroom scare you?"

He looked into my eyes, and what I saw there stopped my heart. "No," he answered. "But, it should scare you."

Chapter Twelve

I jumped up and moved away. "What...what happened to you?"

He smiled bitterly. "What do you think happened?"

"Are you a...vampire?" I asked.

He stared ahead, looking lost. "I don't know what I am. I haven't fed on anyone's blood or anything. But, I can't say the idea doesn't consume me day and night."

I stared at his face, which was much palcr than usual, but hauntingly beautiful. He'd always been nice looking before but whatever had changed him now emphasized everything I'd loved about his features. I had an incredible urge to touch his face, but was a little frightened of what he'd do.

"How did this happen?" I asked.

He leaned back in the chair and sighed. "You remember how Ethan went after us Sunday night and the truck flipped?"

I remembered someone had, but wasn't about to argue about it now. I only nodded.

"Well, you blacked out and I pulled you out of the cab. It was then that Ethan decided to strike."

My eyes widened. "He really attacked you?"

"Yes. Your admirer, or whatever you want to call him, brutally attacked me and left me for dead." He closed his eyes. "He's lucky I was only human at the time because now...I'd rip is throat out," he growled.

I stared at him in confusion, "But how did you end up a vampire?"

He opened his eyes again and the strange light I'd seen in Ethan's eyes was also reflected in Duncan's silver eyes. "Celeste. She found me and brought me back."

"Celeste made you a vampire?" I asked.

He shrugged. "She calls it something else, a Roamer or something. Anyway, I'm certainly not the same physically. Now, I move like the wind and have more strength than I'd ever thought possible. It's like a double-edged sword; both awesome and horrifying at the same time."

I moved closer to him and touched his arm. "What are you going to do?"

He grabbed my wrist and scowled. "You have to quit touching me."

I searched his eyes. "Why?"

He licked his lips. "Because I don't know if I can trust myself around you."

I shook my head. "You...you'd never hurt me."

Not Duncan. Somehow I felt safe with him, even like this.

He stood up. "I should go."

"Wait, are you going home?"

"I don't know. I have this growing hunger and I don't know what I'm capable of anymore. Jesus, Nikki," he said. "I almost lost it on this drunken woman earlier. She'd offered to give me a ride and I... I wanted to tear her throat apart. I could smell her blood. It was..." Tears filled his eyes and he turned away. "I don't want to hurt you," he choked. "I'd never forgive myself."

My heart went out to him. I reached for his hand again but he wouldn't let me touch him. "I want to help you," I whispered. "Stay here tonight, you'll be safe. I just somehow know that you won't hurt me, Duncan."

He looked into the sky and murmured, "I just can't take the chance. Not with you of all people."

I tried a different approach. "Ethan's out there somewhere, and he's much stronger than you because he feeds. You want revenge? Then you either need to feed, which personally, I think is a bad idea for obvious reasons, or hide out until you find a different way to get through this."

He shook his head. "I don't..."

"I know you don't want to hurt me. Just come inside and rest," I urged, pulling him into my warm bedroom.

He relented and smiled sadly as he stared at my mattress. "I would have given anything to have you drag me in here these last couple of months."

I stared up at him and sighed. Part of me still cared deeply for him, but the intense feelings for Ethan confused the hell out of me. I didn't know who or what I wanted. Now, I was half in love with two vampires, which even I knew was insane, not to mention very dangerous.

I tossed a couple of pillows and a blanket at him. "There you go. Now you can rest and we'll talk about it in the morning. I'm staying home from school, by the way. I'll help you get through this."

He sighed and then got down on the carpet, not saying anything.

"Goodnight, Duncan," I said, sliding under my sheets.

He still didn't say anything.

I moved to the edge of my bed and looked down at him. "Duncan?"

He cleared his throat and turned so his back was to me. "Goodnight."

Obviously, I couldn't really sleep with him down there, but I felt like I was doing the right thing. It was my fault he'd been turned into a vampire and I planned on helping him deal with it. As I began sorting things out in my muddled head, I heard a choked sob coming from the floor.

"Duncan," I murmured, going to him.

He turned to me. "Don't. I don't want your sympathy."

"How about my shoulder?" I whispered, putting my arms around his neck and pulling him closer.

"Things are so fucked up," he choked. "All I wanted was to work on boats and be with my dad. It was all that mattered. Then I met you, and..."

Then he met me and I messed up his life, I thought. *Now he's cursed for life.*

"I'm sorry," I whispered. "I shouldn't have dragged you into all of this."

"No," he said, pulling away so we were looking into each other's eyes. "You don't understand. What I was trying to say is...*then* I met you and I didn't care about anything else. I love you, Nikki. You're all I think about. I've missed you so much, and now that I'm one of these... things," he said with a grimace, "we won't ever have a chance..."

I placed my finger on his lips. "Shh... Duncan, don't ever say 'never', okay? There might be a way to beat this and I'm going do everything in my power to help you."

His eyes began to glow brighter and as I stared into them, a wave of intense desire swept through my belly.

"Duncan," I whispered, as he grabbed my hand and brought it to his mouth.

He kissed my finger with his lips, taking a small taste with his tongue. "Oh, God," he groaned, shuddering with pleasure. "You taste so good." Then, he realized what he was doing and tried pushing me away. "No, get away from me."

But my heart was pounding in my chest and I couldn't help myself. I slid my fingers behind his neck and pulled his mouth to mine, hungry for his lips. "Kiss me," I whispered against his closed mouth. "Please."

He moved his face away from mine. "Stop. I'm sorry, I must have done something to you," he said.

But I couldn't stop. Whatever fire he'd ignited was growing and I couldn't help myself. "It's okay, Duncan," I said, touching his lips with my finger, knowing it would be his undoing. "Just let me kiss your lips."

Duncan released a heavy sigh, but gave in. He wrapped his hands around my waist and turned me over until he was on top of me, our bodies pressing together. As our tongues met, I could feel his excitement below pressing up against me. Wanting to feel it closer, I wrapped my legs around his torso but he froze up.

"We have to stop," he gasped, his eyes smoldering with hunger. "Before I lose control."

I slid my hand into his dark, wavy hair. "I've already lost control," I replied, dragging his mouth back to mine.

He kissed me hungrily, sucking on my tongue as I moved my hands over his shoulder muscles and down his back until I reached the curve of his buns. I gripped them tightly in my hands and he groaned against my mouth. "Nikki."

"Duncan," I whispered back.

His cool hands began to move under my shirt, first touching my belly, making me quiver because of the chill. Then they moved to my breasts and the sensation was oddly... exciting.

I gasped.

"You okay?" he whispered.

I nodded and closed my eyes as his hand was replaced by his tongue, which was only slightly warmer.

"You're so beautiful," he whispered huskily.

"Duncan," I breathed, clutching his hair in my hands and pulling him closer to my breasts.

Something happened in that moment. He stiffened up and moved his face away from my skin. "I have to leave," he said, "before I can't stop myself from taking you."

I released a sigh. "You don't have to."

He clenched his jaw. "We're not talking about the same thing. The hunger is magnified being this close to you."

I touched his lips again. "Duncan..."

He moved his mouth away from my fingers. "Stop," he said, staring down at me, his face flushed, his eyes blazing with fire. His mouth opened slightly and it was then that I saw the fangs. "I need..."

"If you need blood that bad," I interrupted, "take it from me."

It was my fault he was a vampire and I felt I owed it to him anyway. I'd already sacrificed myself to Ethan, and I trusted Duncan much more.

"No," he growled. "I'm not going to do that to you."

"It's okay," I said, offering my neck again. I pushed my dark hair away from my neck. "Just take enough to sustain you for a while."

His breathing increased until he was almost gasping. He lowered his lips to my skin, licking just below my ear. I closed my eyes, anticipating the pain from his teeth.

"No," he snapped, getting up from the floor. "What you're asking is suicidal. I have to go."

I reached out for him. "No, please stay."

He stepped towards the balcony without looking at me. "I can't. I knew this was a bad idea."

Then he opened the door and I watched as he leaped over the balcony all the way to the ground and disappeared.

Chapter Thirteen

"Well, that certainly wasn't very smart. He could have drained you down to nothing."

I whipped my head around. "Celeste!" She was sitting outside in the same spot as Duncan had been earlier, staring at me with amusement. "You have to quit sneaking up on people."

She smiled. "Sorry, I didn't want to interrupt your little interlude."

I grabbed a blanket from my room, to wrap around myself. The chill in the air seemed magnified by her presence. I cleared my throat. "So, um where's Nathan?"

She licked her lips. "Oh, he's had an exhausting night. Don't worry, though, he's tucked safely inside of his bed."

My eyes narrowed. "You didn't do anything to him, did you?"

She gave me a wounded look. "You don't trust me very much, do you?"

I didn't answer. Instead, I sat down on the chair next to her and stared off towards the woods, wondering where Duncan was headed. "So," I stated. "You've made Duncan into one of you..."

"I had to do it," she murmured, wrapping a piece of red hair around her finger and staring at it. "He'd lost too much blood."

"Why?"

She raised her eyebrows. "What do you mean, why?"

"Why did you bother saving him? Why didn't you just suck him dry or whatever it is you Roamers do?"

She studied me for a few seconds and then shrugged. "I don't know. I guess I just like Duncan. Besides, I want him to find Ethan and kick his arrogant fucking ass."

"So, it really was Ethan who attacked him?"

She nodded. "Of course, who else could it be?"

I let out a sigh. I was hoping she'd have an answer other than that. "Well, how did you come across Duncan that night?"

She stood up and walked over to the railing. Looking off into the distance, she said, "I was just leaving your house when I chanced upon him. It was a pretty bad scene, though, blood everywhere. Fortunately, I called a couple of my friends and we were able to clear the wreckage before daybreak."

"Why?" I asked.

"It was my dad's idea. He wanted to avoid any kind of investigation."

"I don't understand. If there was blood everywhere, and it's so hard to resist, why didn't Ethan finish him off? Drain him of his blood?"

She shrugged. "I'm really not sure myself."

"Well, what about me? How did I end up back at home?"

"I don't know. You weren't with Duncan when I arrived."

It was getting more confusing by the minute. "What about my father? Was he really here last night? Did you kill him?"

She snorted. "Is that what Ethan told you? That *I* killed your dad?"

"Ethan said there was a man outside of the cabin, watching us through the windows. He said you took care of him."

She threw her head back and laughed. "Oh, he's good."

I raised my eyebrows. "What do you mean?"

"I didn't kill that man, Ethan did. He ripped his throat out and tossed him into the lake, then went after you."

It was hard for me to believe that Ethan had enough time to do that before he'd kidnapped me; but then again, he had unimaginable speed.

"Well, why didn't you stop Ethan? You were outside, supposedly patrolling the area."

She smirked. "Why didn't I stop him? Well, as far as I'm concerned, your father got what he deserved for being a Peeping Tom. Plus, I heard how he abused your mom. You can't be too upset about his death."

"He was still my father," I said, trying to be strong around her even though I was bordering on the edge of hysteria. As horrible as he'd treated my mom, I couldn't help but have feelings for my own father.

"Fathers aren't always what they're cracked up to be," she said. "Just think of it this way, your mom doesn't have to live in fear of him anymore."

We sat in silence for a while as I stared out towards the lake. It was still horrifying to think that my dad's body was lost in there.

"So, now what? Your dad's just going to leave the body in the lake?"

She shrugged. "I'm not sure what dad's planning on doing. He mentioned trying to blame the recent murders on your dad."

I shook my head bitterly. "How convenient."

"It is, actually."

"That's not going to fly with me," I said, sitting up straighter. "Tell your dad that if he frames mine for murder, I'll make waves."

She smiled. "You certainly have balls, I like that. You know what? I'll just let him know you're not tickled by the idea."

"I'm serious. My dad may have been a jerk, but he didn't murder any girls and shouldn't be blamed for it."

"Fine. Well," said Celeste. "I've got to get going. I haven't fed for a while and even you're starting to look interesting."

I gave her a murderous look. "Goodbye, Celeste."

"Goodbye... Miranda," she answered with a funny smile.

I raised my eyebrows. "Miranda? That's what Ethan called me last summer. What's that all about, anyway?"

She laughed. "You still haven't figured it out yet? He never told you?"

"No. I still don't know anything about Ethan other than he's one of you."

She smiled. "Miranda was his wife, Nikki; the love of his life. He's been searching for her for centuries. Now, he thinks he's finally found her."

I raised my eyebrows. "Seriously? Me?"

She nodded. "He's always been obsessed with finding her. All because this old gypsy lady once told him that Miranda would someday return to him."

"And he fell for it? Why?"

"This woman had a knack for telling the future, I guess. I'd never met her but Ethan respected and believed in her so-called … prophecies."

"So, that's why he's so obsessed with me," I muttered. He wasn't in love with me at all. He was haunted by Miranda and consumed with finding her.

"So you see, Nikki, Ethan will do anything for you, only because he believes you're Miranda. If I were you, however," she said, getting ready to jump over the balcony, "I'd stay away from him."

"Why?"

She swung her leg over the railing and looked at me. "Remember the girls who were murdered last summer?"

I nodded.

"Ethan thought they were his dead wife, too. Until he realized they weren't, then he murdered them."

All the blood rushed to my ears as she leaped off the balcony to the side of her truck. I couldn't believe that Ethan was responsible for killing Tina and Amy. How close had I come to being murdered myself?

Chapter Fourteen

It was sometime after four in the morning by the time I'd finally fallen asleep. When Nathan tried waking me for school, I gazed at him with bleary eyes and mumbled that I wasn't going.

He raised his eyebrows. "You're not going? Jesus, I was the one who was up most of the night."

I yawned and slowly sat up. "Actually, Duncan paid me a visit."

His eyes widened. "Duncan? Are you serious?"

"Yes, and there's something I need to tell you."

Just then my mom came up behind Nathan and flashed us a radiant smile. "Hey, kids, you'd better get ready for school, you're going to be late."

"Nikki says she's staying home," said Nathan.

"Oh," she said, walking towards me. She put her hand on my forehead. "Well, you don't seem to have a temperature or anything. You're really not feeling very good?"

I shook my head. "Not really. I think it'd be better if I stayed home, today."

She squeezed my shoulder. "Okay. Well, get some rest and drink some of that orange juice in the fridge."

"Thanks, mom."

"I've got to get ready for work," she said, walking back towards the doorway, her voice a little too bubbly for six-thirty in the morning.

Even Nathan seemed to notice it. "Mom, you're in a very chipper mood this morning," he remarked.

She looked back at us, her eyes sparkling. "Well, I didn't want to tell you this now, I was actually going to wait for dinner tonight, but... what the hell, I'm just so excited I can hardly stand it! Caleb and I are getting married!" she cried and then held out her ring finger to show us the big rock Caleb had apparently given her.

"Wow," smiled Nathan as he grabbed her hand. "Looks like Caleb's doing pretty well as a Sherriff."

She nodded vehemently. "I know, it's a little big, but I'm certainly not going to complain!"

I felt dizzy and sick to my stomach. My mom was marrying a vampire. The only thing worse was her becoming one, and I knew that was next on his agenda.

"Are you okay, Nikki?" asked my mom.

"How can you do this?" I exploded. "You don't even know the real Caleb!"

My mom's face paled. "Nikki, of course I do. He's a wonderful man."

I jumped out of bed. "You can't marry him, mom!" I choked. "He's a vampire! You can't marry a fucking vampire!"

She raised her hands in exasperation. "First of all, watch your language. Now, look, this is getting way out of hand. You need to grow up, Nikki. Stop with these ridiculous fairytales."

"It's not a fairytale, mom! You can't marry him. He kills people and sucks their blood!"

"Nikki, knock it off!" hollered Nathan.

I glared at him. "It's the truth, Nathan! And you knew it, too, before they erased your memory!"

Mom pointed her finger at me. "Enough! I'm going to get ready for work and I'm making an appointment for you to talk to someone about this obsession of yours. This is ridiculous." She then turned on her heel and left my room.

"You are extremely warped," said Nathan, his face red with anger.

"No, I'm not. Duncan was here last night. You can to talk to him about it. He'll confirm everything I've told you!"

"Right," he snorted.

"He will, because Duncan...he's a vampire now, too!"

He laughed out loud. "Oh, here we go!"

"He is," I choked. "Celeste turned him into a vampire to save his life after Ethan attacked him! You'll see for yourself, I swear to God, Nathan!"

He shook his head in disgust. "I'm going to school."

"You have to believe me," I begged as he stormed out of my room.

"Warped!" he called back.

I groaned and pulled the covers over my head. It was so exasperating that nobody believed me! It was then that I made a decision. One that might save my mother's life, before it was too late.

Chapter Fifteen

Feeling calmer now that I'd made my decision, I fell back to sleep and woke up several hours later, feeling much better than I had in days. I went down to the kitchen and fixed myself something to eat. When I finished, I took a shower and then left to go find Duncan. I started with the marina.

"I haven't seen him," said Sonny when I met with him in his office. "I spoke to Duncan on the phone earlier today, however. He said he'll be back in town in a couple of days. I'll definitely let him know that you stopped by."

I nodded. "Thanks."

His lips thinned. "That kid... I'm still pretty ticked off, I tell you. I thought he had more brains than that; nearly gave me a heart attack worrying about him."

I smiled. "I'm sure he didn't realize what he was doing at the time. Duncan would never want to worry you like that, not intentionally," I said.

He shook his head in disgust. "Still, I thought he had more brains that that. It just makes me sick when I think about all of those people who helped me search for him. The time that was wasted and all the turmoil we went through. I still can't believe it."

"I know what you mean. Tell you what, I'll give him hell when I see him, too," I said.

Sonny smiled. "I always liked you, Nikki. You and your brother are a couple of good apples."

"Thanks," I laughed.

"Say hi to your mom for me."

"I will."

After leaving the marina, I decided to drive towards Caleb's house, which was on the other side of town. I'd only been there once, so it shouldn't have surprised me when I took a wrong turn and got lost.

"Crap," I murmured, pulling over to the side of the road. I grabbed my cell phone out of my purse and decided to try Duncan's again. Just like before, however, he didn't answer. I threw my phone against the seat in frustration and closed my eyes.

What am I doing, anyway? This is crazy.

I'd decided to try and kill Caleb myself. I'd read that you could kill a vampire by stabbing it in the heart with a wooden stake. Fortunately, I'd found some narrow pieces of wood in Sonny's marina and had brought a hammer from the garage at home. My plan had been to try and take Caleb by surprise by congratulating him on the engagement. Then, I was going to try and somehow hit him with the hammer until he couldn't move, then pierce his heart with the stake. It sounded so logical earlier, but now, it was completely laughable.

Someone began pounding on my window, surprising the hell out of me. When I saw who it was, I froze up.

"What are you doing in this area?" barked Ethan. He was wearing sunglasses and an angry scowl. "Open the door!"

I swallowed back my fear and unlocked the door.

"I repeat, what are you doing over here?" he asked, getting into the passenger seat.

I bit the side of my lip. "I was searching for Caleb's place."

His lips thinned. "Caleb's? Jesus, you have to stay away from him and the others. It's not safe for a human, especially a young woman like you, to be out wandering around this side of town."

I stared at him, wondering if it was even safe being in a car alone with him. Feeling lightheaded,

I put my hands on the steering wheel for something solid to hold on to.

"Ethan," I swallowed. "So, who's Miranda?"

He stared at me for a minute. "Miranda?"

I nodded. "Yeah, who is she?"

He looked away. "She was someone I knew... a long time ago."

"Do you remember calling me Miranda?"

He smiled bitterly. "Yes, I do. It was a mistake, a slip of tongue. I'm sorry."

"Ethan, did you kill those girls last summer?" I whispered hoarsely.

His clenched his jaw. "I already told you I didn't. Why are you asking me these questions?"

"I..."

Before I could answer, Ethan's door swung open and he was ripped out of the car.

Duncan!

"Get the fuck away from her!" roared Duncan. He pulled his fist back and hit Ethan so hard, he flew backwards and landed several yards away on his back.

Oh crap!

"Duncan!" I yelled, scrambling out of the car. I didn't want him hurt by Ethan.

In a flash, Ethan jumped up and retaliated with his own fists, sending Duncan flying across the field, hitting his head against a large oak tree.

"Stop it!" I yelled.

Ethan turned to me and shrugged. "Well, he started it."

Before I could answer, Duncan was back, body-slamming Ethan to the ground. From there, everything became a blur; all I could see were glimpses of fists flying, feet kicking, and flashes of blood in their frenzied rumble. I stood frozen in horror as the two vampires violently attacked each other, not certain of who was getting the upper hand or who I even wanted to have it.

"Idiots," snorted Celeste, who'd appeared out of nowhere.

I turned to find her sitting on the hood of my car. "Jesus, where did you come from?"

She pushed her sunglasses up and smiled. "I'd been giving Duncan a few lessons on survival when we noticed you and Ethan through the woods. Oh," she cringed, "that's got to hurt."

I turned to see them fighting still, but their movements were so swift, I couldn't tell one from the other.

"Kick his ass, Duncan!" hollered Celeste. "No, not like that!"

Suddenly, I could see both of them and it wasn't pretty. "Stop it!" I screamed, moving towards Ethan, who, although his face was a smear of blood, was now standing and had Duncan by the throat. He was squeezing it so hard, that Duncan's eyes were bulging out of his red face. I tried grabbing Ethan's arm, but he was too powerful. "Please," I cried. "Ethan! Stop this!"

Ethan's face was a mask of red rage.

"Ethan!" I repeated.

He looked at me and swore. Then, he released Duncan, who toppled to the ground. "You're lucky," he growled. "If it wasn't for Nikki..."

"What?" rasped Duncan. "You'd try to kill me again?"

"Kill you? I don't know what the hell you're talking about," hollered Ethan, his nostrils flaring.

"You're nothing but a coldblooded killer, a pariah," spat Duncan. "But you know what? Someday I'm going to kill *you*."

Ethan laughed sardonically. "You don't have a chance in hell with someone like me. You have no idea who you're messing with."

"Keep talking," growled Duncan, his eyes full of hate. "Because soon you'll be silenced forever."

Soon they were both neck to neck, glaring at each other, like two boxers in a ring, ready to pounce on each other.

"Would you both just stop!" I pleaded. "You're both acting like idiots!"

Duncan was the first to back down this time. He turned to me and held out his hand. "Come on, Nikki. I'll drive you home."

"You just don't get it, do you?" growled Ethan, moving to my side before I could answer.

He put his arm around me possessively. "She's mine."

"Get your hands off of her," snapped Duncan. "Nikki's afraid of you. You're a murdering psychopath!"

Ethan laughed. "I don't have time for this nonsense. You're Celeste's little pet now, anyway. You're hers just as much as Nikki is mine!"

"What are you talking about?" I snapped, now moving away from Ethan. I didn't like the way he was treating me.

Ethan turned to me. "It's obvious that Celeste changed him into a vampire."

"Well, that doesn't make him hers, does it?" I asked, glancing at her.

Celeste smiled, but didn't say anything.

Ethan smirked. "They bonded. The only way to change someone into a vampire is by having intercourse and sharing each other's blood."

I looked at Duncan, whose face was filled with anguish. "Duncan?"

"I don't even remember it," he said, shaking his head. "I swear, I don't."

Celeste frowned. "That's absurd, of course you do."

"I don't," he repeated. "I was injured and I barely remember anything that's happened the last few days."

"Well, you must have remembered the other times," chuckled Ethan.

"The other times?" I asked, more than a little confused.

Celeste walked over to Duncan and put her hand on his arm. "Yes," she smiled. "It takes three 'bondings' to become a vampire. The third time was right after I found him injured near your cabin."

I stared at him in horror. "You had sex with Celeste three separate times?"

"I swear I don't even remember any of the times, Nikki. I don't."

Just then a squad car turned down the road and headed towards us. The top lights began to flash and Celeste smiled. "Oh, here comes daddy. Stick around, Ethan; I'm sure he has some interesting questions for you."

Ethan reached for me. "Nikki, come with me," he said.

I stepped away from him. "No."

Duncan stepped towards me and held out his hand. "Nikki doesn't belong to you, Ethan," he said. "Come on, Nikki, I'll take you home."

I shook my head. "No, Duncan. I'm not going with you, either."

Then, before I changed my mind, I got into my car, started the engine, and took off.

Chapter Sixteen

It was after seven by the time I made it back to the cabin.

"Where were you?" snapped my mom when I walked through the door. "I've been trying to call you all afternoon."

"Sorry, I think my phone battery died." I stepped past her and towards the staircase. "I needed some fresh air, that's all. I'm exhausted now, I think I'm just going to go and lie down."

"You shouldn't have gone anywhere, young lady!" she hollered as I proceeded up the stairs. "You're still grounded and supposedly sick!"

I didn't answer her; instead, I went into my bedroom and closed and locked the door. When I turned around, Ethan was waiting for me on the balcony.

Crap.

We stared at each other for a minute, until he gave me one of his disarming smiles and I eventually gave in.

"I knew you couldn't resist," he teased as I let him in.

"What do you want?" I asked, surprised to see that his face was completely healed without any hint of being in a fight.

He lay down on my mattress and folded his hands under his head. "This is nice," he sighed. "I haven't slept in a real bed for days."

I raised my eyebrows. "I thought you guys preferred coffins?"

He burst out laughing. "Coffins? You shouldn't believe everything on television."

I sighed. "Ethan, I think you should leave."

He turned on his side and rested his head in his hand. "I have a better idea, why don't you come over here and keep me company?"

I shook my head. "I don't think so."

He gave me a pouty look. "You're no fun."

I sat down on a chair and stared at him. "Tell me the truth; did you attack Duncan the other night?"

He frowned. "I already told you the truth."

I crossed my arms under my chest. "Well, both of them said it was you."

In a flash he was crouched in front of my chair with his hands on the arms, blocking me in. "I'm telling you the truth," he said, staring into my eyes. "I wouldn't lie to you."

"Are you trying to hypnotize me again?" I whispered, leaning back.

His eyes filled with anger. "No, dammit, I'm being honest with you. I didn't do anything to Duncan the other night. I wasn't even in town."

"Well who did?" I asked, staring in wonder at his eyes, which were so clear and blue, they reminded me of an ocean beach. "And who's been killing all of those girls?"

He moved closer until our faces were only inches apart. "I don't know," he whispered, staring down at my lips.

"I..."

The next thing I knew, he'd captured my mouth with his and I forgot about everything else, even Duncan. Soon, his tongue was inside, touching and exploring; sending a wave of heat throughout my body. I slipped my arms around his neck and sighed as he lifted me out of the chair and brought me to my bed.

"I want you," he whispered huskily, setting me down. "I can't wait anymore."

I couldn't speak.

He kneeled next to me on the mattress and removed his shirt, tossing it to the floor, revealing perfectly sculpted muscles and a narrow waist. I reached up and touched his chest, which was hard and smooth under my hands.

"Nikki," he whispered. "Tell me if you want this to stop anytime. I don't want to force you into anything."

I licked my lips. "No, I don't think I'll want to stop."

His lips curled up into a smile and then seconds later, they returned to my mouth, this time with much more intensity. I moaned against his lips as his hands began to move under my shirt.

"I can't stop thinking about you," he whispered, his lips moved to my neck. "You've put some kind of spell on me."

I gripped the sheets as his tongue traced a hot trail down to the junction between my breasts. When he couldn't go further, he lifted my shirt away from my body and threw it down to the floor. Then he unclasped my bra, freeing my breasts.

"So beautiful," he said, cupping them in his hands. When I thought it couldn't get any better, his warm mouth came down and captured my nipple, rolling it around with his tongue.

"Oh," I gasped in pleasure.

He chuckled and began teasing both of them, until I was whimpering and pulling at his hair. He raised his mouth and I could see the tips of his sharp teeth. He took a deep breath and released it slowly. "Your scent is driving me wild. I have to...be careful."

My body was on fire and I didn't care what he did anymore, as long as it meant being close to him. I wrapped my legs around his waist then slid my arms over his pants and cupped his firm buns. Soon he was pressing against me with his pelvis and I moaned with desire.

"Nikki," he growled, sliding his hands under my butt, pulling me even closer. "I need you. God, do I need you."

"I want you," I breathed.

His eyes burned into mine as he began unzipping my jeans. I closed my eyes and tried to relax as they slipped away from my legs. Soon, he was kissing me again while one of his hands began caressing my thighs. As it moved closer to my panties, my legs began to tremble.

"Do you want me to keep going?" he whispered, moving his hand to the edge of the fabric.

"Yes," I squeaked.

His hand slid underneath the material and when he touched the hot junction between my legs, I gasped in pleasure.

"Ethan," I moaned, as his fingers began to move. "Oh..."

His mouth returned to my nipple, sending even more sensations to the place his fingers were also attending to.

"Nikki," he breathed, as his fingers moved faster, driving me crazy. "Say my name."

"Ethan."

After a few seconds, my stomach muscles clenched up and something inside of me seemed to burst, sending shock waves all the way down to my toes. Tears filled my eyes and I didn't know whether to laugh or cry.

He noticed the tears and kissed my cheeks.

"I'm sorry," I whispered, not understanding all of my emotions.

"Don't be sorry," he murmured, sliding my panties off. "That's supposed to happen."

"Oh."

I watched as he removed his pants and then blushed. When he was naked, lying next to me, I began to tremble again.

"Don't be afraid," he whispered, sliding his hands back to my thighs and parting them. "I'll be gentle."

I smiled and he lowered his mouth to mine, kissing me deeply. I began to lose myself again, consumed by passion and something even deeper.

"I can't wait anymore," he groaned, kissing my neck.

"Then don't," I whispered, opening myself up.

He positioned himself, staring into my eyes as he began to push. It took a few motions until he was able to enter and I gasped at the hot pain which quickly disappeared. Soon, we were moving together and his eyes began to glow with the fiery light I'd seen before.

"Oh, God, Nikki," he growled, moving faster. "You feel so good. I won't be able to...last..."

I closed my eyes as his mouth found my neck again, expecting his teeth to puncture the skin. But it didn't happen. Instead, he began to groan as I moved my hips with his and then, after a few more thrusts, he tensed up and shuddered above me.

"Are you okay?" I whispered, staring into his eyes.

He kissed the tip of my nose and then my lips. "I'm definitely okay." Then he fell on top of me and wrapped me in his arms.

Chapter Seventeen

I woke up the following morning with the *Kings of Leon* telling me that "my sex was on fire." I shut off my alarm and that's when all of the memories of the previous night came rushing back.

Holy crap, I was no longer a virgin!

I'd had sex with a vampire!

A vampire who'd disappeared during the night. My fingers went to my neck and I sighed with relief. No bites.

I closed my eyes and thought about Ethan. God, the things he'd done to me, not once, but several times during the course of the evening, just left me breathless. Good thing my mom's bedroom was far enough down the hall that she hadn't heard a thing.

Our lovemaking had been earth-shattering and wonderful beyond belief, but it had also been totally suicidal. I'd given myself freely to someone who could have just as easily made a meal out of me. As I began beating myself up about being so naive, there was a knock at my bedroom door. "Honey, are you awake?"

Shoot, I was still naked!

"Yeah, hold on!" I jumped out of bed and grabbed a robe out of my closet, then took a deep breath and let my mom in. "Hi."

Her eyes narrowed. "Are you feeling okay? You slept for a very long time."

I stared at her innocently. "I'm great. I feel so much better."

She looked over at my bed, which was a tangle of sheets and blankets. "Oh, looks like you had a little period mishap sometime during the night."

There was a small amount of blood on the sheets. My cheeks turned crimson. "Oops."

She went over to my mattress and pulled off the sheets. "It's okay; I'll throw them into the wash before work."

"Thanks."

"So," she said, removing the linens. "Are you going to school today?"

I nodded.

"Good. I'd like to take you both to dinner tonight since we didn't get a chance to yesterday."

I nodded. "Okay."

"Better get ready for school," she said, leaving my room.

I took a shower, slipped on a charcoal V-neck sweater dress, tights, and black suede boots. I pulled my hair into a loose up-do and then went down to breakfast.

"You must be feeling better," said Nathan, who was sitting by the counter next to mom, eating a large bowl of cereal, "haven't seen you in anything other than your ratty old jeans lately."

"Ha ha," I said, looking into the fridge. I grabbed the bottle of orange juice and began filling a glass.

"Oh, no," murmured my mom, who was at the counter, watching the news.

I turned around to look at the television and froze. A photo of my co-worker, Susan, flashed across the screen.

"Early this morning the body of nineteen-year-old Susan Fields was found in a dumpster behind Ruth's Diner on Main Street," said the reporter.

I dropped my glass and it shattered. "Oh, my God," I choked.

"No!" gasped Nathan in horror.

"Officials aren't saying whether this is related to the other teens found murdered

Saturday morning, but obviously foul play is suspected. We'll keep you updated as more information is released."

My mom turned off the television while Nathan and I stared at each other in shock. Both of us knew Susan fairly well; Nathan had even gone out with her a few times.

"I'm so sorry," sighed mom. "I know you three were friends."

I turned to my mom with tears in my eyes. "I think I'll be staying home again." Then I stepped over the broken glass and went upstairs to my room. I threw myself onto the bed and buried my face into my pillow, mourning for the first friend I'd made in Shore Lake.

Seconds later, Nathan knocked on the door and entered, his face full of anguish. "This is really fucked up," he said, running his fingers through his hair. "I just saw her last night, too."

I turned to him. "You saw her last night?" I sniffled.

He nodded. "Yeah, after work I was craving an omelet. They have the best egg dishes, you know, especially the Texas style, with the peppers and..."

"Yes, I know..." I prodded, impatiently. "Keep going."

He nodded. "Okay, anyway, I sat up at the counter and we talked for a while. Then, some guy walked into the diner and she pretty much shut me down."

I raised my eyebrows. "What do you mean, shut you down?"

"She basically cut me off during our conversation to go and wait on the other dude. I could hear her gushing over him with the other waitresses, too," he scowled. "I was like… hello, what am I, scrap-meat?"

"What time did you leave the diner last night?"

He shrugged. "About ten o'clock."

"Did you notice anything else?"

He shook his head. "No, the place was pretty dead, except for that other guy. I do remember she talked to him quite a bit, though."

"I wonder if Rosie knows anything more."

I also wondered who that guy was that Susan had been talking to. Something niggled at the back of my mind. Then it hit me.

"I wonder if it was Drake," I said.

"Who's Drake?"

"A guy she dated a while back. A friend of Ethan's. I'm pretty he's a vampire, too."

He snorted. "Of course."

I sighed. "Nathan, when are you going to start to believe? Too many people are dying around here, and if you can't accept what's going on, you're putting your own life in danger."

He sat down at the edge of my bed and looked down at his hands. "Well, to tell you the truth, I've been having some strange... I guess you could say... visions or dreams."

"What do you mean?"

He shrugged. "Just... I don't know. Ever since I went to the club with Celeste the other night, I've been having these nightmares. But the crazy thing is they seem so real."

"What kind of nightmares?"

He smiled sheepishly. "Well, I um...I had this dream that I was chasing Celeste through the woods and when I caught her, I..."

"What?"

He frowned. "I hate to say this but, I held her down and tore into her throat, like a freaken vampire. Thanks, by the way, for putting those ideas in my subconscious, with all your vampire talk."

"Nathan..."

He stood up and began to pace. "The shitty thing is..."

"What?"

He smiled humorlessly. "I can't believe I'm actually telling my own sister this, but it kind of excited me."

I raised my eyebrows. "Oh...that is pretty creepy."

He snorted. "Yeah, tell me about it."

I took a deep breath. "Nathan, have you had sex with Celeste?"

He stared at me for a minute and then gave me a shit-eating grin. "Yeah, once."

I stared at him in horror. "Did she bite you?"

He shrugged. "No, not that I know of."

I moved over to him and tried looking at his neck. "Let me check."

He pushed me away. "Oh, for the love of God, she didn't bite me, okay? She's not into freaky sex or anything; at least not with me."

"This is serious, okay? We need to check for bites."

"Fine. If it'll get you off my back, check for yourself."

I examined his neck but didn't seem to find anything.

"Are you sure she didn't bite you? Maybe somewhere else?"

"Well, actually, now that you mention it, she scraped my back."

I raised my eyebrows. "With her teeth?"

He smiled. "Yeah, but don't ask me to get into details."

I raised his T-shirt and examined his back. Sure enough, right below his shoulder blades, were two little holes. "Oh, my God," I groaned. "She bit you."

He stood up and went over to the dresser mirror. "Yeah, looks like she did." He smiled. "She's a little tigress in bed."

"That's gross and T.M.I., Nathan. You have to stay away from her. I'm serious."

He dropped his shirt back down. "Now why would I want to do that?"

"If she bites you three times during sex, you'll turn into a vampire."

His eyes lit up. "You mean I might get lucky two more times?"

I punched him in the shoulder. "You're such a pig. Look, this isn't joke. She already turned Duncan into a vampire. Have you seen him yet?"

His eyebrows shot up. "Duncan's back in town?"

"Yes and she had sex with him."

He clapped his hands and laughed. "Holy crap, Duncan had a shot at her, too?"

I grimaced. "Nice."

His face fell and he put an arm around me. "I'm sorry. I forgot you and Duncan had something going last summer."

"Well, it's not even that. Duncan says he doesn't remember much of what happened anyway. She probably put some kind of spell on him."

"Right, a spell. Well, I definitely remember having sex with her. She didn't need a spell to get me naked."

I glared at him. "Obviously. My point is, if she's bitten you once already, she must have real plans for you."

He bit the side of his lip and looked thoughtful. "Tell you what... let me speak to Duncan about all of this. It kind of pisses me off that she's playing both of us. I mean, shit, we're good friends."

"Yeah, if you can find him."

He shook his head. "She really had sex with Duncan?"

I nodded. "I guess so."

He sighed. "Shit."

Chapter Eighteen

We both missed school that day, and while mom left for work, we snuck out and took a trip into town. Our first stop was the marina.

"Hey, Sonny, Duncan around?" asked Nathan as we strolled into his office.

Sonny frowned. "Aren't you supposed to be in school?"

Nathan nodded. "We are, but one of our friends was murdered last night. Did you hear about Susan?"

His face turned somber. "I saw that on the news this morning. I still can't believe it myself, that poor child."

"Obviously, someone's killing these girls and we're trying to find a way to help with the investigation," said Nathan. "In fact, I actually saw Susan last night at the diner."

His eyebrows shot up. "You did? Well, I'm sure the sheriff will be interviewing everyone she came in contact with yesterday. Better let him know you saw her, too."

"What time did Duncan come home last night?" I asked.

"He got back into town pretty early this morning. He's probably still sleeping."

I looked at my watch; it was almost ten in the morning.

"Do you think he'd mind if we stopped over?" asked Nathan.

He shrugged. "Go for it. The house should be open. Tell him to get his ass to work, I need him here."

"No problem," said Nathan. "Come on, Nikki."

Duncan and Sonny lived in an old house right next to the marina. We walked over and rang the doorbell, but nobody answered.

"Let's go inside," said Nathan, pushing the door open.

"Do you know where his bedroom is?" I asked, as we stepped into the living room.

He shook his head. "No. I'm surprised you don't."

I smacked his shoulder. "Very funny."

He laughed. "Why don't I check upstairs and you look on the main floor?"

"Okay."

I made my way through the house, which was definitely a bachelor pad. Empty beer bottles and soda cans were sitting out, along with some empty bags from a fast food joint up the street. The place looked like it hadn't been vacuumed in forever, and the kitchen floors were sticky.

They could use a maid, I thought with a grimace. I was sure Sonny was bringing in good money with the marina, although from what Nathan mentioned, he was pretty tight with it.

I moved past the kitchen and noticed there were a couple of rooms down the hall. I knocked on the first one, but nobody answered, so I opened it slowly.

"Duncan?" I whispered, stepping inside.

The shades were pulled, so it was dark, but I could see him sprawled out on top of his bed, wearing only a pair of black and white striped boxers. He appeared to be sleeping with earphones from his iPod still attached to his head. The music was coming through loud and I was surprised that anyone could sleep that way.

"Hey," I said, squeezing his arm.

His eyes popped open and he stared at me as if I was a complete stranger.

I smiled. "It's just me, goofball."

The next thing I knew, he let out a strangled growl and I soon found myself underneath him with his hands on my throat, squeezing. He bared his fangs and I stared at him in horror, waiting for him to rip out my throat.

I opened my mouth and tried to scream, but it was painfully impossible with his hands squeezing. Just when I thought my life was over, he seemed to snap out of it.

"Nikki?" he choked, releasing my neck. "Oh, God..."

"What the fuck?!" hollered Nathan, rushing into the bedroom. "Get off my sister, man!"

Duncan got up and I rolled away, wheezing and coughing.

"I'm so sorry, Nikki!" cried Duncan, his eyes full of remorse. "I didn't know what I was doing... I'm...God, I'm so sorry!"

Nathan helped me off the bed. "Are you okay?" he asked, pulling me into his arms.

"Yeah," I whispered, although my throat was pretty sore.

"What the hell, Dunc?" snapped my brother above my head. "Are you out of your freaking mind?"

Duncan grabbed a pair of jeans from the floor and pulled them on. "I'm sorry. I must have been still sleeping or something. You know I'd never hurt her; not intentionally."

"Jesus, remind me never to invite you over for a slumber party," said my brother as he released me. "You scared the shit out of us, bro."

Duncan moved towards me and touched my cheek. "I am so sorry, Nikki. You know I'd never try to harm you on purpose. You know that, right?"

I nodded. I realized it probably had something to do with being a vampire but I vowed to never wake Duncan up from a deep sleep ever again.

"Come here," he said, pulling me into his arms. "I can't believe that happened. I feel like such an asshole."

I let him hold me, although I couldn't get the image of his attack out of my head. Then, when I felt how warm his body was, I pushed him away. "You've fed," I whispered hoarsely.

He brushed his dark hair from his eyes and stared at me but wouldn't say anything. I noticed that his face had more color than the last time I'd seen him and his eyes were even more of a vibrant silvery-gray. Thinking of him feeding from a living person gave me the chills.

"You've eaten?" asked Nathan. "Shoot, I was going to take you out for breakfast at Ruth's Diner."

Duncan turned towards my brother and smiled. "I had a late night snack, but I could certainly join you guys. I'll meet you in the living room in a few. Just let me get ready."

I followed Nathan back to the living room, still feeling shaky.

"You really okay?" he asked,

I nodded. "I'm fine, but obviously Duncan isn't. He's warm to the touch."

Nathan raised his eyebrows. "And...that's not fine?"

I shook my head. "No, it means he's fed. He's had blood."

He sighed. "Nikki..."

"Ready to go," interrupted Duncan, now wearing a khaki colored sweater, a pair of brown suede boat shoes, and dark sunglasses.

"Yeah, I'll drive," said Nathan.

I was silent as we walked to the car, although Duncan tried grabbing my hand a couple of times. I brushed it away and then stuffed my hands into my jacket pockets. I still couldn't get over the fact that he'd fed and now that Susan was murdered, it made me wonder. Was he responsible for her death?

Nathan, on the other hand, was talking a mile a minute about Susan and the news report.

"I can't believe she's gone, man," he said in a strangled voice. "I actually made out with her a few times last summer. She was a sweet chick. Shit, I feel sick to my stomach thinking about what might have happened to her."

"Yeah," murmured Duncan, who was sitting in the passenger seat so I couldn't see his expression. "What a waste. I didn't know her very well, but she seemed nice."

When we arrived at the diner, it was busy, as usual. We seated ourselves at a booth in the corner and Duncan slid in next to me.

"Hi, kids," said Rosie, handing us menus. "You hear?"

I nodded. "Yeah, that's why we're here and not in school."

There were tears in Rosie's eyes. "She was a good kid," she murmured. "I can't believe she's gone."

"Me neither," I said. "Whoever did this, I hope they find him and hang him by his balls. He's doesn't deserve the air he breathes."

"It's not safe for anyone with this psychopath on the loose. You be extra careful, Nikki," said Rosie. "He seems to be going after young girls around your age."

"You say he, maybe, it's not even a guy," said Duncan.

We all looked at him.

"I'm just saying," he said, playing with the sugar packets. "It could be a female. Don't count a woman out."

I glanced at Duncan and wondered if he knew who'd killed Susan. It wouldn't have surprised me if it was Celeste. Unfortunately, I couldn't read anything in his expression because of his sunglasses. I reached over and snatched them from his face.

"Hey," he said, trying to take them back. "I was up late and my eyes hurt."

I scowled. "Tough. Have some manners."

He sighed and looked up at Rosie. "Sorry."

She smiled. "It's okay. Can I get you guys something to drink right away?"

Nathan and I ordered sodas and Duncan ordered a glass of water.

"How's your wrist?" she asked me.

I raised and moved it around. "Better. I meant to call you, actually. I can start back whenever you want me to. It's a little tender, but I'm sure it'll be fine."

She nodded. "Hate to ask but, how about tonight?"

I nodded "Yeah, sure, what time?"

"Four?"

"I'll be here," I answered.

"So," said Nathan, after she left. "Duncan, I have some questions for you."

Duncan's look was stoic. "What's up?"

Nathan leaned forward. "First of all, what the hell is going on with you?"

Duncan rubbed a hand over his chin and smiled bitterly. "Had a rough week, man."

"So I hear," replied Nathan.

"Tell him," I prodded Duncan. "Tell Nathan, because he doesn't believe me."

"Tell him what, exactly?" he asked, turning towards me.

My jaw dropped. "You're kidding me, right?"

"Let's start with Celeste," said Nathan. "What's going on between you two?"

Before Duncan could respond, Ethan walked into the restaurant with a blond woman. With his long, black leather jacket, sunglasses, and lazy grin, he reminded me of a musician who'd just gotten done pulling an all-nighter. If that wasn't shocking enough, when the woman turned around, my blood turned to ice. It was the nasty woman from the other day, Faye Dunbar.

"Oh, my God," I whispered, as Ethan removed his sunglasses and led the woman over to the other side of the diner. They sat down in a booth together, face to face. She had a flirtatious grin on her face, and from the sensual smile on his face, he also appeared to be enjoying her company. Then, when I saw him grab her hand and place it in his, I wanted to throw up.

"What the hell?" I hissed, clenching my fists as Faye leaned forward and kissed Ethan's lips; the same ones that had been all over my body only hours before.

Nathan turned to see who I was staring at and almost choked on his water. "Holy shit."

"Let me out, Duncan," I demanded, my blood boiling.

"Don't," he said, holding my arm. "You don't want to disturb them. In fact, that woman isn't who she appears to be."

I stared at him. "What's that supposed to mean?"

His face darkened. "I met her yesterday."

"Yeah, well, I met her a few days ago. She's an arrogant bitch," I said.

And now she was with Ethan! What the hell was going on?

Duncan's eyes moved to Nathan and then back to me. "She's a very powerful shape-shifter. Don't fuck with her."

"A what?" I whispered.

"A shape-whater?" asked Nathan.

Duncan sighed. "Her name is Faye and from what I've been told, she is not someone you want to mess with."

"First of all," smiled Nathan. "You're both insane; seriously, insane. Second of all," he said, turning towards me. "Nikki, it's obvious that Ethan and this woman have something going. So, just get over whatever it is that you feel for him and grow the fuck up. He's a no-good asshole who obviously, likes a variety of women. He's a little too old for you, anyway."

I shook my head. "You don't know what you're talking about."

"I agree," said Duncan. "Stay away from him. You're just a toy to that guy and Faye, well, you need to avoid her at all costs. She'll kill you without a second thought if you make her mad."

I looked back over to Ethan's table and our eyes met. The shock registered on his face was priceless. He quickly turned away.

"He just saw you, obviously," said Duncan.

"I want to go over there," I mumbled. "Duncan, move please."

He sighed and got out of the booth. "You're making a mistake by interrupting them. I can tell you that right now."

I took a deep breath and let it out. "Listen, I just don't want him to think that I'm bothered by them being here," I said, although I was mad as all hell. "I'm just going to go over and say hello, that's all." Then I reached up and gave Duncan a kiss on the mouth, hoping that Ethan had witnessed it. I knew it wasn't fair to Duncan, especially since everything that had happened, but I wanted Ethan to know that I wasn't anyone's play toy.

Duncan stared hard at me for a moment and then nodded. "Okay. Just be careful."

I turned away and began moving towards Ethan, whose face darkened considerably when he saw me coming.

I gave him the coldest smile I could muster and his eyes narrowed.

"Well hello, there," I said, approaching their table.

Ethan stared at me like I was a complete stranger and said hello ever so politely.

"Oh, are *you* working today?" asked Faye, an irritated look on her face. "How lovely."

Then, as clear as day I heard her voice in my head.

Not this little irritating bitch, again. Fuck!

"Excuse me?" I said. "Did you just say something? Because I could have sworn you just called me an irritating bitch."

Faye looked at me in surprise and then flashed an angry scowl at Ethan. "You did not touch this girl, did you?"

Ethan licked his lips but didn't say anything. He picked up the menu and started to examine it.

Her hand snaked out and grabbed his wrist. "Ethan?" she hissed. "Did you?"

He glanced at me and then turned back to her. "She's nothing, Faye; just needed to regroup one night when I was weak. It was obviously a mistake."

I stared at him in horror. I felt like he'd just kicked me in the heart.

"Bastard," I whispered hoarsely, my eyes filling with tears.

"Leave us," said Faye with a bored look on her face. "Before I call the manager over and place a complaint against you."

I turned away and stormed towards the bathroom, needing to "regroup" myself. I was on the verge of having a major crying attack and wasn't about to do it around everyone in the restaurant.

"You okay, Nikki?" asked Rosie as I rushed by her.

"Something in my eye," I mumbled.

When I reached the bathroom, I hurried into the stall and only then allowed myself to cry.

I was a mistake, he'd said.

I cried rivers of tears, flushing the toilet several times to drown out the sound of my sobs. Fortunately, nobody else walked in.

I was a mistake...

I'd never felt so betrayed and heartbroken in my life. Before we'd had sex, he'd told me that he loved me. Now that he'd gotten what he'd wanted – sex – he was being cruel and heartless. Although he was a vampire, his actions were so...strangely human. I now realized that he was just a cold bastard and I vowed to never let him confuse me or control my desires again. If he showed himself to me again, I was prepared to tell him to where he could stick his teeth along with something else.

A knock at the door stopped my ranting.

"Nikki?" called Duncan. "Are you okay?"

I let out a ragged sigh. "I'll be out in a second, Duncan!" I called.

"Okay. I'll be out here waiting for you."

I moved to the sink and washed my face with cold water. Unfortunately, my eyes were puffy and I knew there was no way I could hide the fact that I'd been crying. I frowned in the mirror and dried my face.

"Duncan," I said, stepping out of the bathroom. "Can I borrow your sunglasses?"

He reached over and touched my cheek with his fingertips. "Are you okay?" he asked.

I tried to smile, but I'm sure it came out sour. "I'm fine," I lied.

He lifted my chin. "Don't let him do this to you. He's not worth it. Okay?"

I nodded.

Duncan grabbed my hand. "Come on."

We walked back to the table and there were three plates of food already sitting there.

"I ordered for you," said Nathan, stuffing his face with mouthfuls of hash browns. "Hope you don't mind. I'll eat whatever you can't."

"Thanks," I said, glancing towards Ethan's table. Fortunately, they were now gone.

"Yeah, they left," said Duncan, noticing my interest.

I slid into the booth and began picking at the omelet Nathan had ordered for me. I wasn't hungry and the thought of food at that particular moment actually made me ill.

"Okay, spill it," said Nathan, his mouth full of food. "Both of you have a lot of explaining to do. Give me all you got, include whatever vampire fantasy you have in your head, too, just in case I'm wrong."

I smiled. "Just in case?"

He shrugged. "I haven't seen any proof of vampires at all. Or shape-shifters. By the way, that's even more unbelievable, I have to say."

Duncan put a hand over the one Nathan had resting on the table. "Fine, Nathan," he nodded. "You want proof? I'll give you proof."

Then, Nathan and I stared at Duncan as he opened his mouth.

"What the fuck?" whispered Nathan, snaking his hand away from Duncan's grasp. "What the fuck is wrong with your teeth?"

"I'm one of them now," answered Duncan. "And believe me, it wasn't by choice."

"You had those implanted," smiled Nathan. "That's a little weird, dude."

Duncan looked at me and shook his head. "Hey, I tried. He's just too stubborn to open his mind to other possibilities."

I bit the side of my lip and smiled. "There's another way to show him."

Duncan nodded. "I know, but we're not outside and I'm not very good at it, yet."

"No, that's not what I mean," I said. Then, I grabbed the back of Duncan's head and pulled him towards me, kissing his lips. He answered me hungrily, wrapping his arms around me, pulling me in closer.

"Oh, for the love of God," grumbled Nathan. "This isn't the time or place for you to start making up. Get a room or something."

Duncan was practically groaning as I kissed him in the booth and the noise in the diner seemed to quiet down considerably. Soon there was an uncomfortable silence.

"Stop it," snapped my brother. "This is fucking embarrassing."

I pulled away. "Look at his eyes," I breathed. "Nathan, look at them."

Duncan's eyes were smoldering and burning yellowish-red with the familiar fire of vampire lust. There was nothing human about it.

"Holy shit," whispered Nathan.

"That's not all," I told my brother. "He can probably fly like the wind and he's fast... so... fast, Nathan. He even took on Ethan yesterday."

Duncan grinned. "Yeah, I held my own pretty good. Of course, Ethan is hundreds of years old, and obviously, I have a lot to learn about being a vampire."

"You mean a Roamer?" I said.

Duncan shrugged. "Whatever the hell I am now."

Nathan put his fork down and stared at us, unhappily. "Okay. You've got my attention, now. What else you got?"

Chapter Nineteen

We decided to drive to Caleb's house to talk to Celeste. Duncan still claimed he didn't know anything about Susan's death but ventured that she might.

"So, where did you get the blood to feed?" I asked Duncan, after we'd settled back into Nathan's car. "It's pretty obvious that you fed."

"Yeah, so fine, I fed," he said, looking out the window of the Mustang. "I had to."

"On who?" asked Nathan. "You didn't kill anyone, right, bro?"

He shook his head. "No."

"Well, then how did you get it?" I asked, still thinking about Susan and how he'd attacked me earlier. I wasn't certain that he even knew if he'd killed anyone after that episode.

Duncan ran a hand over his face and then turned back to look at me. "Listen, I didn't kill anyone, okay? I wouldn't kill another human being. Ever."

"How then?" I asked, crossing my arms under my chest.

"I went to Club Nightshade," he mumbled, turning back towards the window. "There are a lot of willing girls hanging out there, ones that will do anything you want. It's pretty dark and disturbing, actually."

"You hooked up with a chick at Nightshade last night?" laughed Nathan. He stuck a knuckled fist out towards Duncan to smack. "Way to bring it, Dunc!"

Duncan ignored his fist. "It's nothing to be proud of. In fact, I didn't even want to feed, but I was weak and if it wasn't for Celeste, actually, she was the one who dragged me there."

"Celeste," I muttered. "She seems to enjoy dragging you to all kinds of places."

Including her bed...

He shrugged. "Yeah, well, I can't argue the fact that she did save my life. After your buddy, Ethan, attacked me."

"He's *not* my buddy," I snapped. "Besides, you had sex with her three times. Twice, before you were even injured."

Duncan turned back to look at me. "I told you, I don't even remember the first two times. I swear to God, I really don't remember anything."

"I have to go with Nikki on this one," chuckled Nathan. "How can you not remember being in bed with Celeste? I mean," he shook his head. "Come on."

"She's a vampire," he answered. "Obviously, she can manipulate people to do whatever she wants."

"What about you?" I asked. "Can you manipulate people to do your bidding now?"

He turned back around and smiled devilishly. "I don't know, care to find out?"

From the look on his face, I knew he wasn't joking around. I could feel my own face heat up.

"Duncan, who do you think killed Susan?" asked Nathan.

He turned to him. "I don't know. I suppose it could be any of the vampires living at Caleb's. Celeste says the others are getting antsy and much more volatile."

"She told me they don't like to stay in one spot for too long," I said. "I wonder how Caleb works that out, being a cop and all."

"I'm sure he's very convincing at his job interviews," said Duncan.

"How many vampires actually live out at Caleb's?" I asked.

"Seven, I think, including Caleb and Celeste," said Duncan.

We drove the rest of the way in silence and I tried not to think of Ethan, but it was next to impossible. I hadn't even realized how much I'd wanted him, until today. Now that he'd basically stabbed me in the heart, I felt hollow and ashamed of my own weaknesses. I should have known that crushing on someone who wasn't even human was setting myself up for certain doom.

As if reading my thoughts, Duncan turned around. "Are you doing okay, Nikk?"

I nodded.

He stared at me for a second and touched my leg. "Don't be so hard on yourself. Falling for Ethan wasn't your fault. Even I understand that now."

I gave him a weak smile and he squeezed my knee.

When we arrived at the large colonial mansion, it seemed so ominous, even in the daylight. We sat in the car and stared at it.

"What are we doing here again?" asked Nathan, rapping his knuckles on the steering wheel.

I swallowed. "Finding answers."

"Come on," said Duncan, getting out.

We got out and followed Duncan up the porch. Before we could even knock, however, the front door opened.

"Well, what an interesting surprise," purred Celeste. She appeared to be wearing nothing but an oversized hot pink T-shirt that left little to the imagination. Her long, red hair was loose and she looked like she'd just enjoyed a tumble in someone's bed. I wondered if the vampires fooled around together when they weren't hunting humans.

"Obviously, it wasn't too much of a surprise," said Duncan, pushing past her, into the house.

"Hi, Celeste," grinned Nathan, staring appraisingly at her outfit.

I scowled. From the look on my brother's face, he was still putty in her hands, vampire or not.

Ignoring me, she locked her arm through his and I followed them into the house. "I missed you, Nathan," she said, giving him a pouty look. "You never called me back."

"We've been busy. Did you hear about Susan?" he asked.

Her eyes widened. "Yes, what a shame – I went to school with her last year."

"She was a nice girl," he said.

"I'm sure," said Celeste.

I followed them to a large sitting room, where Duncan was already seated and looking pensive.

"You okay?" I asked him.

He shrugged. "Just still trying to absorb everything, you know?"

Celeste looked at him and then turned towards Nathan. "So, he told you everything, I take it?"

Nathan nodded. "Yeah. Got to say, it's a little hard to believe."

She smiled. "You're not frightened?"

He paled slightly. "Should I be?"

"No," said Caleb, entering the room. He was dressed in a long, blue robe, his hair tousled, like he'd also just woken up. "You have nothing to fear; not from me or Celeste, at least."

Nathan's eyes narrowed. "Does our mom know what you are?"

Caleb's lips turned up. "No, not yet. But soon, she'll know everything."

"Yeah, soon when you decide to change her into a vampire completely," I snapped.

He studied me for a minute and then let out an exasperated sigh. "I don't know why you're so against her...surviving. She's an extremely sick woman. This is the only shot she's got to stay alive."

"How can you be sure?" I said, clenching my fists. "What about chemotherapy? What about seeking medical help, instead of being condemned to living a life where you have to drink blood and stay out of direct sunlight?"

"It's not so bad. In fact, life has many rewards when you're a Roamer. I'm sure you've figured out some of these already, hanging around Ethan," he answered with a small smile.

I blushed at the knowledge in his eyes and looked down.

"Okay, I'm extremely lost," said Nathan, moving away from Celeste. "Are you trying to say you're going to change our mother into a...vampire?"

Caleb turned to Nathan. "As I've explained to Nikki, your mother has cancer. The moment we connected, if you want to call it," he said with a sad smile, "I sensed it. The worst thing is, that it's terminal, Nathan. She won't survive another two years without my help. She'll just wither away... and die."

Nathan's face fell. "What? Did she tell you this? How do you know?"

"She doesn't even know. Not yet," he answered.

"What if he's lying?" I said to Nathan. "What if he just wants our support to help him with mom?"

"That's absurd," snapped Caleb. "Why would I go to that extreme, just to turn your mother into one of us?"

"To get our support," I repeated. "So we won't try and stop you."

His eyes flashed. "I don't need your support. Have you talked to your mother lately? She's happier than she's been in a long time. She suffered the abuse your father put her through for many years and now I'm trying to give her everything a woman like her deserves. When I offer her this gift, I doubt she'll refuse it."

"This gift of yours, it sounds pretty morbid to me," I said.

Nathan ran a hand through his hair. "This is some heavy shit. I don't even know what to say."

"Nathan," said Celeste, putting her arms around his waist. "Everything will work out for the best, I promise. Your mother will live and we can be together."

"Excuse me, Celeste," I hissed. "Do you mean you and Nathan or you and Duncan?"

"Yeah, I'm a little curious about that, myself," muttered Nathan.

She gave us both a bewildered look. "Oh, for the love of God! I saved Duncan's life! That was the only reason we bonded."

I scowled at her. "What about the two times before he was injured?"

She threw her head back and laughed. "You're unbelievable," she said. "You're acting like a jealous innocent virgin, yet you're stringing Duncan AND Ethan around. You of all people shouldn't be pointing fingers."

"This isn't getting us anywhere," interrupted Duncan, his eyes filling with anger. "We came here today to find out if you know what happened to Susan."

"To be truthful, we really don't. Have you asked Ethan?" replied Caleb.

I shook my head. "No. But I doubt very highly that it was him."

Caleb frowned. "Why?"

I took a deep breath. "Because we were together, until early this morning."

"As I was saying..." said Celeste, under her breath.

I stole a glance at Duncan and could see his anger. I felt horrible, especially now that I was beginning to realize how much he still cared for me. I decided to change the subject.

"Who and what is Faye?" I asked.

Caleb turned back to me. "Why?"

"Because she was with Ethan this morning at the Ruth's Diner."

"Stay away from her," said Caleb. "She's very dangerous."

"What is she?" I repeated. "Duncan said she's some kind of shape-shifter?"

Caleb nodded. "She has the power to change form as well as manipulate people. Not only is she a shape-shifter, but she also feeds on humans. I'm not talking just the blood, either."

I grimaced. "What's going on between her and Ethan?" I asked.

Celeste smiled. "Probably just sex. He's a very promiscuous guy, Nikki. I could have told you that from the beginning."

The pot calling the kettle black, I thought.

Just then, another young guy entered the sitting room. He was tall with longish, sandy blonde hair and bright green eyes. He also looked like he'd just gotten out of bed and wore nothing but a pair of black velour drawstring pants.

What was with all the hot vampires?

"What's going on here?" he asked Caleb, "A party, mate? And I wasn't even invited?"

I recognized the Australian accent and knew right away; it had to be Drake, the guy Susan had gone out with a while back. Looking at his chiseled muscles and sexy grin, I totally understood how she'd been drawn to him.

Caleb cleared his throat. "Friends of Celeste's. They were just leaving."

"Oh, no! Don't leave on my account," he smiled, staring at me with interest. "I just blew into town and would love a little fresh company."

"Did you hear about Susan?" I blurted out.

His eyebrows shot up. "Susan?" he asked, studying my face.

"Yeah, the waitress you were talking to in the diner last night?" snapped Nathan. "The one you were flirting with?"

Drake frowned. "I wasn't in any diner last night, sorry, cobber."

My brother scowled. "The name is Nathan and yes, I did see you last night talking to Susan. Right before she was murdered."

Drake's face darkened. "I don't know what the hell you're talking about. I just got into town early this morning."

"Bullshit," said Nathan.

Drake stepped forward until he was in Nathan's face. "You callin' me a liar, *cobber*?"

"I guess I am," snapped my brother, his jaw clenched. "*Fucker.*"

Celeste got between them. "Okay, that's enough. Cool your jets."

"I have to agree," said Caleb. "There isn't time for this, and Nathan," he smiled, "I wouldn't start picking any more fights with Roamers. Your mother would kill me if I let anything bad happen to you."

Duncan stepped forward and patted Nathan on the back. "Let's get out of here, come on. They're not going to give up one of their own. This was a wasted trip."

Although they were both still staring at each other with obvious rage, Drake and Nathan stepped away from each other.

"This really was a waste of time," I huffed. "Obviously, nobody here is going to admit to anything."

Drake, who seemed to have already forgotten his beef with Nathan, sidled up to me and smiled. "I'll admit one thing, Ethan has very good taste."

"What do you mean?" I asked, staring at his amused expression.

"When he thought you were in danger, he dropped everything to come back here to Shore Lake. Christ, you were all the bloke talked about in New York City. It was getting bloody annoying," he said, touching a strand of my hair. "But now," he smiled. "I guess I can understand his interest."

Nathan grabbed my arm and pulled me away. "Okay, enough. Let's get the hell out of here."

"Goodbye, Nathan," called Celeste, as he pushed me through the doorway. "Don't forget about tomorrow night. Call me!"

Nathan glanced back and shook his head as we left the house. "I don't like the way that asshole was looking at you. With our luck, he'll be trying to pick up where Ethan left off."

"Oh, crap," I said. "I hope not."

"I wish these vampires would just leave our family alone," he mumbled.

"Even Celeste?" I asked as we reached the car.

He scowled at me over the roof of his Mustang. "Yeah, even her."

"Um, so, what did she mean about tomorrow night?"

"I told you we were going to Club Nightshade Friday night. But, I doubt I'll be going back after all of this bullshit."

"I don't blame you," I said. "Stay away from her, Nathan."

"Wait up!" called Duncan from the top of the porch. A fraction of a second later, he was standing next to us by the car wearing his sunglasses.

"Dude," cried Nathan. "How in the hell did you do that?"

Duncan shrugged. "I guess I don't really know."

I looked at my watch; it was getting close to three. "We have to get back to the cabin. I told Rosie I'd be back at the diner at four."

"Chill out, we'll make it," said Nathan.

"Can you drop me off at the marina?" asked Duncan as we pulled away from the mansion.

"No problem, bro."

I sat in the back and stared out the window, thinking about everything that had happened in the last couple of days. Duncan had turned into a vampire, I'd lost my virginity to one, and tomorrow, my mother was going to Vegas and would surely return as one of them. It was a living nightmare.

"What are we going to do about mom?" I asked, biting my thumbnail.

"I've been thinking," said Nathan. "That she needs to know the truth, and now that Duncan's a vampire, he can back us up."

"I'll help as much as I can," he said.

"What if she really has cancer?" I asked.

"If she does, then mom can decide what *she* wants to do. Not give the choice to some creature of the night, no offense, Duncan."

He smiled and shook his head. "None taken."

Nathan turned on his iPod and cranked up a recent song he'd downloaded by "Train." I closed my eyes and listened to the lyrics, wishing I could escape the mess we were in. "You know," I hollered after a while. "I think Caleb really loves her."

Nathan turned down the music. "Yeah, well, so do we, and our intentions are good. I'm not so sure about Caleb's."

Chapter Twenty

We dropped Duncan off at the marina first.

"I'll see you tonight," he said, as I got out of the car to hop into the front seat. "I think we should talk, too."

I sighed. "Duncan, you know, I really need some time to think about everything. My head is spinning right now."

He grabbed my hand and I noticed his was getting cool again. "I don't expect anything from you," he said. "I just have a few things that I'd like to get off my chest."

I stared at his face, which seemed much paler than earlier. "Duncan, your skin, it's getting cold."

He frowned and he released my hand. "Yeah, I know."

I sighed. The thought of him having to drink blood to stay alive for the rest of his life made me physically ill. Not to mention how he'd actually acquired it the previous night. "What are you going to do?"

He licked his lips and looked away. "It's not your problem."

"Duncan," I whispered.

He shook his head and stepped back. "I'll see you later." Then, before I could say anything more, he was gone in a flash.

"Jesus," said Nathan as I got in next to him. "That speed of light shit is really unnerving."

"Actually, he's getting weaker and needs to feed again," I mumbled.

Nathan swore under his breath.

"We have to help him," I said. "There's got to be some other way. Duncan is so sweet, I'm sure this whole thing must be driving him insane."

"I tell you one thing," said Nathan. "I'm not going near Celeste anymore. The hell if she's biting me two more times. I don't care how hot she is."

"Thank God. I'm so glad you finally believe me."

"Yeah. I feel like an asshole now, giving you so much shit before."

"Hey, you said it, not me."

When we arrived, home, I quickly changed into my uniform and grabbed the car keys.

"You sure you don't want a ride?" asked Nathan. He was in the kitchen eating a big bowl of ice cream.

"No, I'm sure I'll be fine," I said. As I watched him eat, I knew he'd never make it as a vampire. He'd drive a stake through his own heart if he couldn't eat pizza or cookie dough ice cream anymore.

"I wonder..." I murmured.

"What?"

"I wonder if piercing a wooden stake through a Roamer's heart would even kill them. They don't appear to be afraid of crosses, holy water, or garlic. Celeste told me that those were all bogus assumptions."

He snorted. "Well, they'd definitely go down if you cut off their heads, I'd bet anything on that assumption."

"You're talking zombies," I said. "You're supposed to cut off their heads and that stops them."

"Zombies, vampires, hell, I'm sure it would work with either."

I shook my head. "I can't believe we're even having this conversation."

He grabbed the ice cream out of the freezer and proceeded to refill his bowl. "No shit."

"We should probably figure out how to kill them, just in case."

He nodded solemnly. "Yeah. Come home as soon as you can. I'll make sure mom doesn't slip out to Caleb's house again after she's done with work."

"Okay."

"Call me if you need anything!" he hollered as I left the cabin.

Rosie was ecstatic when she saw me walk through the front door of the diner. "Thank God," she said. "I need a cigarette and we've been swamped all day."

"How's your wrist?" asked Darlene, who was one of the older waitresses.

I moved it around. "A little tender but... I think I'll be okay."

Darlene nodded. "Good, because it seems like we've had many more people stopping in today, now that Susan's gone. I think folks are curious about what happened to her and think they might find the answers here."

I nodded. "I guess I don't blame them. God, I'm going to miss her," I said, my eyes misting over. "She was such a sweetheart."

"Same here, honey. Coming, Hank!" she hollered towards an older customer who was holding a cup in the air.

We were busy the entire evening and by the time nine o'clock arrived, both my feet, as well as my wrist were sore.

"Go home and put ice on that wrist of yours," said Rosie, studying my wrist at the end of my shift.

"I will," I said.

She patted me on the back. "Thanks for coming in tonight, Nikki. I really appreciate it."

I nodded. "Looks like you're going to need to hire someone soon."

"I know. This is getting ridiculous; first Amy and now Susan? I'm going to have to hire bouncers to walk you girls to your car. In fact, I'll have Herb do it right now if you'd like?"

Herb was her husband and the fry cook. He was also a former Marine and built like a linebacker. One who'd retired twenty years ago but still kept himself in pretty decent shape.

"I'll be fine," I said. "My car is right under the light over there," I pointed.

"Just be careful," she said.

"Did you want me to come in tomorrow?" I asked.

She shook her head. "I'm closing the diner after lunch. Susan's family is having a special memorial service for her around four o'clock. You should go, it's at Saint Odelia's," she said.

"Yeah, I'll be there," I said, pulling on my jacket.

She patted my arm. "Okay, kid. I'll see you tomorrow."

I walked to my car and noticed that it was beginning to snow. Shivering, I started the engine and grimaced when it hesitated.

Crap, I'd forgotten to have Nathan look at it.

Saying a silent prayer, I took off down the road and started driving back towards the cabin, watching in awe as the snowflakes grew larger. Since I'd lived all of my life in San Diego, I wasn't used to snow and couldn't wait to have my first white Christmas.

Beautiful, I thought, staring at the intricate patterns of the flakes as they dissolved onto my windshield. My mother had told me once that no two were alike, and as I watched the crystal-like flakes flutter down, I smiled at their beauty.

It normally took me a good twenty minutes to drive home from work and I turned on my stereo to listen to some music. It was then that something farther up the road caught my eye. As I drew closer to the dark shadow, I noticed it was a rusty old Buick pulled over to the side of the road. I thought the car seemed vaguely familiar, and an image of a girl in my grade with long, brown hair and glasses suddenly popped into my head.

Taryn Cooper?

The lights were on and the driver's side door was wide open, but I didn't see anyone in the vehicle. I pulled around it and stared into my rearview mirror, wondering what I should do.

I grabbed my purse and started searching for my phone to try and call Nathan; he'd know what to do. When my phone appeared to be missing, I swore at my stupidity. I'd set it on the charger at home, and had forgotten to bring it along.

Crap.

I got out of my car and walked over towards Taryn's vehicle. When I noticed her purse abandoned on the front seat, more alarm bells went off in my head.

Who'd leave their purse?

I stepped back from the car and stared towards the woods, wondering if she'd ventured into them. I wasn't sure why she would, but I hadn't seen her on the road walking towards town, either, and I doubted she'd walk the opposite direction.

The silence of the night was broken by a shrill cry. "Help!"

Heart pounding, my head whipped around to the trees on the other side of the road. The voice seemed to have come from that direction.

"Help, me! Please!"

I'm not even sure why I started running towards her cries; it was probably the stupidest thing I could do, but I couldn't seem to stop myself.

"Taryn?" I hollered.

"Help!"

I rushed towards the sound of her voice, wishing I'd grabbed something to defend myself with just in case, like the wrench Nathan had placed in the back of my trunk.

"Taryn!" I called, slowing down as I entered through the tall trees. It was dark and difficult to see with the moon offering very little light. I began walking deeper into the woods, now petrified that I'd made a very bad choice, but still unable to turn away from someone needing help.

A strangled cry from behind a large oak tree stopped me in my tracks. Swallowing the lump in my throat, I slowly moved around it.

"Oh, my God," I choked, staring at the grisly scene on the other side. It was definitely Taryn, or what was left of her. She lay on the dirt, staring lifelessly at the sky with her throat sliced open and blood oozing from the wound.

"Taryn," I whimpered, backing away in horror, expecting whatever had attacked her to come after me next. Out of the corner of my eye, I noticed a shadow skirting around the trees and my heart stopped.

Scared out of my mind, I turned around to flee, but something heavy landed on me, slamming me to the ground.

"No!" I screamed in horror as my eyes locked with a pair of vivid yellow ones.

"Yes!" growled the monster, holding me down with its crushing weight. It raised a sharp, pointy claw and pressed it against my throat.

"Please," I squeaked, feeling the claw rake over my skin. "Let me go…"

"Stupid fool," it breathed, licking its putrid lips. "Very stupid."

I tried to turn my head to keep from smelling the foul stench coming from its mouth. It reminded me of rotten meat and copper pennies.

"Look at me, girl…" it hissed.

I whimpered as the creature gripped my neck and forced me to meet its unholy gaze. As it stared at my face, its mouth twisted into a smirk. "Ah…I… know… you…"

I stared at the monster, whose face reminded me of some kind of reptile, with green scales, wormy lips, and freaky snake-like eyes. I definitely did not know this demon.

"Lucky…" it hissed, releasing its vise-like grip on my neck. "Oh… you are so… lucky… I will let you live… to suffer…but only… for now…"

Then, as clear as day, the word "bitch" echoed in my mind and my breath caught in my throat.

Faye.

Her lips curled into an evil smile, then she leaped into the sky, but not before I caught a glimpse of her gargoyle-like body, with wings that must have measured well over twenty feet.

Stunned that she'd actually let me go, I pushed myself up off the ground and then ran like hell back to my car.

Chapter Twenty-one

"Where were you?" barked Nathan when I stormed through the cabin door. "I was about ready to send out a search party!"

"Oh, my God, Nathan!" I choked, rushing towards him. I threw my arms around my brother and wept.

"What's wrong?" he asked, patting my back.

I looked up at him. "I...I just found a dead body!"

His eyebrows shot up. "What?"

I brushed my wet cheeks. "It was Taryn Cooper," I said, my voice shrill. "Faye killed her and then she went after me."

"How'd you escape?" he asked incredulously.

I moved away from him and began to pace. "She actually let me go and said I was lucky, this time. You should have seen her," I said, wrapping my arms around myself. "She looked like some kind of dragon or reptile. It was horrible."

He closed his eyes and groaned. "Fuck. I can't deal with any more of this shit right now. I feel like at any minute, I should be waking up from this nightmare."

I grabbed a tissue from the coffee table and blew my nose. "I know. I wish that's all it was."

He walked over to the window and looked out into the darkness. "I knew we shouldn't have moved here. I just had this feeling that it was a mistake. With our luck, dad will show up next, and that would be the least of our worries."

My heart stopped. I'd forgotten to tell Nathan about our dad, his body tossed somewhere in the lake.

"Hey, Nathan, where's mom?" I asked, deciding to tell both of them at the same time.

He turned around and sighed. "She went to Caleb's. I couldn't stop her."

My jaw dropped. "Nathan, what the hell?"

He ran a hand through his hair. "I know. I tried to keep her here, but she said that he needed her. I even tried to tell her about the vampires."

"What did she say?" I asked.

"She told me to stop listening to you or she'd send both of us to a shrink."

I shook my head. "This is bullshit. We have to talk to her before she leaves tomorrow."

"You try and talk to her then," he mumbled. "She won't listen to me."

"She'll believe us if Duncan can back us up. Where is he?"

He shrugged. "I don't know. He said he'd be over a while ago and he never showed."

"Okay, we'll wait for him and then drive over there," I said. "I'm going upstairs to take a quick shower and change my clothes."

Nathan didn't respond, he just sat down on the sectional and put his head in his hands.

"Once Duncan gets here, everything will work out," I told him. "You'll see."

He nodded.

I really didn't believe it would be that easy, but I could tell he was on the verge of having a nervous breakdown. So was I, for that matter. We had to keep it together, at least for mom's sake.

I sighed and then went upstairs to take a shower. As I stood in the shower washing the conditioner out of my hair, images of Taryn's mangled body swept through my mind. I couldn't get the picture of her lifeless gaze out of my head and it was all I could do to keep from going hysterical. The fact that I'd almost been killed by whatever the hell Faye had turned into wasn't easy to digest, either. As far as I was concerned, we all needed to leave town as quickly as possible, especially after hearing Faye's threats. Without a doubt, I knew she had plans for me, and there was no way I wanted to stick around to find out what they were.

I turned off the water and then opened the shower door for my towel. After drying my skin, I put on a robe then leaned over to wrap the towel around my hair. As I lifted my head back up, I was met with two piercing blue eyes.

"Jesus!" I gasped, backing away from him. "Don't do that!"

Ethan smiled wickedly. "Do what?"

"Sneak up on someone getting out of the shower," I snapped, pulling my robe in tighter.

He stepped towards me and tugged playfully at my robe. "Looks like you're finished, which is too bad. I'd have loved to join you."

I slapped his hand away. "Don't touch me!"

Ethan moved towards me again, this time until he had me backed up against the tiled wall. "Your mouth says 'no'," he whispered, staring at it. "But your eyes say something entirely different."

I stared up at him. "Get the hell out of my house."

He raised his hand and touched my cheek. "Come on, don't be like that."

I raised my chin. "Do you think I'd just let you waltz in here and do whatever you want with me after what you said at the diner earlier?"

His eyes softened. "I'm sorry. I know it was rotten, but I did it for your own good."

My eyebrows shot up. "Excuse me?"

"I was trying to protect you," he said, turning away. He walked out of the bathroom and I followed him.

"What do you mean?" I asked.

He sat on my bed and began removing his shoes. "Faye is dangerous."

"So, I've heard. Is that psycho creature from hell your girlfriend or something?" I asked, watching him unbutton his shirt. He wore black dress pants and a dark blue shirt that brought out his eyes more than ever.

"Or something," he said, reaching for me. "Look, I didn't come here to talk about her. I came here to be with you."

I slapped his hands away again and stepped back. "You're incredible."

He leaned back against my pillows and gave me a slow, sexy grin. "You told me that quite a few times last night. Come join me on the bed and I'll give you an encore."

I raised my hands in frustration. "Just stop, Ethan. There's no time for this. Faye murdered someone I knew from school tonight and she came after me, too!"

His face darkened and he sat up. "What?"

I told him about my encounter with Faye and he stood up. "Shit," he said as he began to pace around my room.

"You have to control your little concubine, or whatever the hell she is," I said. "I'm not ready to die."

He stopped pacing and stared at me. "I can't control her," he said. "Nobody can. But, I'll protect you. In fact, we need to leave this place before she comes back for you. Right now."

I stared at him incredulously. "I'm not leaving with you, Ethan."

He grabbed my arms and stared into my eyes. "I'm not asking you this time, I'm telling you. We're leaving."

Before I could protest anymore, my balcony door opened and Duncan walked in. "Let her go," he growled, his eyes blazing with fury.

Ethan released me and snarled. "This is none of your business. Leave us!"

Before I could comprehend what was happening, Duncan launched himself at Ethan and they crashed onto my bed.

"Stop it!" I yelled as fists began to fly.

"What in the hell?!" hollered my brother as he stormed through the door.

"It's Ethan and Duncan!" I cried, stepping back as Duncan was kicked across the room. He landed against the wall but quickly launched himself back towards Ethan, who was already prepared for another attack. I watched in horror as his fist slammed into Duncan's face, and blood sprayed all over my purple and green comforter.

My new comforter!

"Stop!" I screamed as Duncan opened his mouth and bit Ethan in the shoulder, adding more gore to my beloved bedroom linens.

Nathan grabbed my arm and pulled me out of the room. "Let's get the hell out of here," he said.

"But what if one of them gets really hurt?" I hollered, pulling away.

"What if you get really hurt?" he yelled. "Let's go!"

But I was far too worried about Duncan and Ethan. I turned to charge back into my room when Nathan picked me up and threw me over his shoulder. "Dammit, we're leaving...now!" he grunted.

I punched him in the back. "For the love of God, put me down!"

He ignored my protests and rushed down the stairs while I continued to struggle and break free. As he got to the front door, he put me down. "Jesus," he said, trying to catch his breath. "You need to lay off the pie at work."

I glared at him. "This isn't funny, none of it is."

He put his hands on my shoulders and gave me a stern look. "Listen, I know you're pissed, but we have to go and check on mom. She called me a few minutes ago and seemed pretty upset. I'm really worried about her."

I stared at him in shock. "I didn't know. Let's go."

He stared down at my robe and swore. "You need something to wear. Check the dryer, I think it's full."

I ran into the laundry room, which was next to the kitchen right underneath my bedroom, cringing at the loud banging and growls coming from up above. I was not looking forward to inspecting the damage in the room later.

Bending down next to the dryer, I grabbed a pair of blue jeans and a green sweater, and then slipped them on as quickly as possible. As I turned to leave, I noticed the house was now completely silent.

"Come on!" hollered Nathan, from the entryway.

I flew out of the laundry room and ran smack into Ethan. His lip was bleeding and there was blood on his shoulder where Duncan had bitten him.

"Going somewhere?" he asked, smiling grimly.

I nodded. "Yes. Where's Duncan?"

He snorted and shook his head. "Duncan, that fool. He's beginning to really piss me off."

I glared at him. "Just answer me, is he alive?"

"Pretty much."

I nodded. "Okay, good. We're leaving to check on my mother."

"The only place you're going is with me," he said, grabbing my arm. "I have to keep you safe."

I tried freeing my arm from his grasp but he only tightened it more.

"Ethan, this is ridiculous. I can't go anywhere with you," I said. "My mom might be in danger."

"I'll check on your mom once you're hidden. But right now, all I care about is making sure you're out of Faye's radar."

Before I could protest, he picked me up in his arms.

"Stop it," I demanded. "You can't do this..."

"Put her down," barked Nathan, who was now blocking our path in the hallway. "Or I'm going to have to hurt you."

Ethan chuckled. "I like your spunk. Now," he said, his eyes growing hostile, "get out of the way. I'm only going to ask you once."

"Put my sister down, you son-of-a-bitch."

"Oh, so you've met my mom?"

"Don't be an asshole."

"Move."

"Fuck you."

Ethan's face hardened. "Don't say I didn't warn you."

The next thing I knew, he repositioned me over his shoulder, slammed Nathan against the wall like a football, and then took off out of the cabin with me as his captive, once again.

Chapter Twenty-two

"Nikki," murmured Ethan.

We were in a small cabin, nestled somewhere deep in the woods. I had no idea where we were, exactly, but it appeared to be falling apart and pretty much abandoned. When Ethan noticed me shivering, he'd started a warm fire in the small fireplace.

"Nikki," he repeated, stepping away from the fire.

"What?" I snapped.

He sighed. "I know you're angry, but I'm doing this for your own good."

I crossed my arms under my chest. "I'm not a child, you know. I should be able to make my own decisions instead of being carried around like I'm only two years old."

He stepped over to where I was sitting, by a small round table pushed into the corner of the room. He knelt down next to me and took my hand. "You're not a child, but you need protection. Quit begin so petulant."

I snatched my hand back. "Quit kidnapping me."

His eyes lit up. "Secretly, I think you enjoy it."

I raised my chin. "You're obviously wrong."

He touched my neck. "Oh, I don't know...your pulse is racing."

I glared at him. "That's because I want to murder you right now."

"Liar," he whispered. Then, he lifted me up from the chair, grabbed the back of my neck, and pulled my mouth to his.

"Mm...no..." I murmured, pushing against his chest. When that didn't work, I locked my lips together until he pulled away, an amused expression on his face.

"Don't fight it," he murmured, his eyes burning with fire. "Give in to your emotions."

I set my jaw. "The only emotion I have now is rage. Now, before I follow your advice and seriously punch you, help my mother. Please, you promised me you would."

"First, give me a little more incentive," he said, cupping one of my breasts.

I slapped his hand away and glared at him. "You're incorrigible," I muttered.

He grabbed the back of my hair and pulled it to the side, exposing my neck. He slid his tongue just below my ear and down to my collarbone, nipping playfully at my skin. "I've been thinking about you all day," he whispered. "I've never wanted anything as much as you. Hell, my hunger for you far surpasses my thirst for... other things."

Feeling a rush of heat between my legs, I forced myself to focus on the issue at hand. "Please," I begged. "We're running out of time."

He groaned and then released me "Okay, fine. But I expect a nice reward when I get back."

"Ethan, I swear to God, if you save my mother, I'll give you anything you want."

His lips twisted into a devilish grin. "I'm going to hold you to that."

I swallowed. "I'm serious; I'll do whatever you ask."

"I wouldn't expect anything less."

I raised an eyebrow.

He brushed away some dust that had settled on the mantle and cringed. "Sorry about this mess. You should be safe here, though. The gentleman who owns this cabin never comes here in the cool months."

I looked around and noted the entire place was lacking any kind of cleaning, even in the summer months. Still, if he said I was safe, I wasn't going to argue. "Okay. Hurry back though, I don't like being all alone out here."

"I will. I'll make sure your mom is safe then I'll come back for you. I'm looking forward to exploring these promises you've made."

I blushed. "Okay."

He stepped closer and brushed his lips on my neck and whispered, "I'm going to make you forget about everything else in this world, including Duncan."

"Ethan," I said, pulling away. "What happened to Duncan anyway?"

He scowled. "He's fine. Probably licking his wounds, which, could have been a lot worse; I was easy on him."

I didn't think he'd been easy on him at all. In fact, I figured the only reason Ethan hadn't killed Duncan was because he knew I'd never forgive him.

As if he could read my mind, he said, "I only kill when I have to, or when someone threatens those I care about. Duncan is just a fool who needs to learn a few lessons, one being that you're mine, and I'll strike down anyone who doesn't respect that."

The way he was looking at me gave me the chills. "I'm yours?"

His eyes traveled down the length of my body. "Yes, Nikki, every inch of you is mine, and if you haven't noticed, I'm very selfish."

I licked my lips. "Oh."

He opened the front door and turned back to look at me. "You belong to me and God help anyone who tries to stand in my way."

Then, in a flash he was gone, leaving me hot, breathless, and as always, worried.

Chapter Twenty-three

I sat at the table and stared outside into the darkness. It seemed like it had been hours since Ethan had left the cabin and I was now terrified that something very bad had happened. He was immortally fast and this was taking much too long. Several times, I considered leaving, but something inside of me urged me not to. There were many things lurking in the darkness around Shore Lake and I would be easy prey. For now, I would continue to wait; at least until daylight. As I stared at the moon and thought about the night's events, my eyelids began to get heavy, and eventually I nodded off.

"Nikki," whispered a soft, feminine voice into my ear.

I opened my eyes and raised my head from the table.

"That sleeping position doesn't look very comfortable," teased Celeste.

I wiped a little drool from my chin and cleared my throat. "What are you doing here?" I asked.

She sighed. "Ethan sent me here, there's been a problem and I'm supposed to bring you to him."

"A problem? What about my mother?" I asked. "Is she okay?"

Celeste nodded. "Your mom is fine. She's with Caleb."

I wasn't sure how fine that was, but at the moment, I had no other choice but to leave with Celeste and go to Ethan. I licked my lips. "Okay."

She grabbed my elbow. "Come on, we must go quickly."

I stood up and followed her to the door. "How did you get out here anyway?"

She smiled. "I drove."

I sighed in relief. "Good, because I'm getting tired of all this flying."

"Not your thing, huh?"

"Yeah. Makes me too dizzy. I'd hate to throw up all over you."

She cringed. "Well, it's a good thing I drove then."

It was still dark as we stepped off of the porch and walked to the car.

"Where'd you get the Mercedes?" I asked, admiring the pearly white vehicle.

"Oh, it's my dad's. He just purchased it recently," she said.

"So," I said as I got in and she started the engine. "What's happening?"

"I'm not at liberty to say. He just told me to bring you back into town. He'll tell you everything."

"In town?"

She nodded. "Yeah, we're supposed to meet him at Club Nightshade."

"Isn't that place closed at this hour?" I asked, looking at the time. It was just past three in the morning.

She smiled. "It's okay. We know the owner."

"So, have you talked to Nathan or Duncan?"

She shook her head. "No... I um...haven't spoken to either of them."

I ran a hand through the tangles in my hair and studied her profile. Her red hair was curled and every piece looked strategically placed. She always looked perfect. It was annoying as all hell.

"Seriously? Neither of them showed up at your house?"

She shrugged. "Tell you the truth I haven't been home much. So, I guess it's possible that one of them may have made an appearance."

"Oh."

"Music?" she asked.

I nodded and she turned on the radio.

As she cranked up a song from Green Day, I stared blindly towards the woods, thinking about Taryn and how terrified she must have been as Faye hunted her down and finally ended her life. It was a horrible way to die.

"I found a body tonight," I said over the music. "A girl from school."

Celeste turned down the radio. "Really?"

I nodded and looked at her. "I know it wasn't any of your Roamers, though."

She gave me a teasing smile. "You sure about that?"

"It was definitely Faye who killed her. It wasn't pretty."

Her eyebrows went up. "Really?"

I shuddered. "It was horrible. She ripped the poor girl's throat out."

"And, how do you know it was Faye?"

I told her what had happened and she frowned. "I wonder why she allowed you to live. It doesn't sound like her."

"All I know is that Ethan is set on keeping me hidden and as far away from her as possible."

"Why?"

I smiled. "I guess he sort of likes me."

She snorted. "Yeah, I'm starting to get that."

I sighed. "Celeste, do you know what's going on between him and Faye?"

"Ethan? Well, he's Faye's boy-toy."

My eyebrows shot up. "Excuse me?"

She shrugged. "What don't you understand? Ethan belongs to Faye and she doesn't like to share."

It was becoming very obvious to me that none of these creatures liked to share.

"So, they're lovers?"

Celeste smiled. "They're more than that. They've known each other for centuries. You can't come between something like that."

I stared at her, wondering how she knew so much about their relationship. "So, she would be pissed if he fell in love with someone?"

"Ethan doesn't know what love is," said Celeste, with a smug smile. "He likes the thrill of the chase, but once he thinks he has you, it's over. Not only will he break your heart, but he'll eventually kill you in the end."

I brought my hand to my throat, where his lips had been earlier. "He'd kill me?"

"If he wouldn't, she definitely would. In fact, if Faye knew there was something going on between you two, she'd skin you alive."

I stared out the window. "She's a monster."

Celeste didn't say anything, just turned up the radio and continued to drive. As we entered the town, it seemed ominously quiet. The club, on the other hand, was still lit up and going strong.

"Here we are," she said, pulling into the parking lot. She parked on the side of the building and turned off the engine.

"Wow, I thought they'd be closed by now," I said.

"I think there's some kind of after-party."

"Oh."

She grabbed her purse. "Let's go."

I'd passed the impressivcly designed building many times driving through town but hadn't given it much thought. I wasn't into clubbing, and from the rumors I'd heard about the place, I was better off not knowing what went on behind the doors of this particular place.

"Amazing, isn't it?" breathed Celeste, as we walked through the parking lot.

"Lots of willing donors for you in there I'll bet," I mumbled.

"You have no idea," she replied with a smirk.

We walked up the steps where a bald-headed, muscular bouncer opened the doors for us. "Hey, Celeste," he said, holding the door open for us.

"Hey, Trevor," she replied, brushing past him.

Trevor gave me a once over and nodded. Not sure what to do, I nodded back.

"Follow me," hollered Celeste over the booming music, which only grew louder as we walked down the long mirrored hallway. When we reached the main level of the club, I was stunned. Hundreds of people were on the dance floor, grinding and moving against each other, as if they were all alone in their bedrooms.

"Whoa," I said, stopping in my tracks, having never experienced anything quite like it.

She turned to me and smiled. "I know, right? It's fucking beautiful."

I didn't know about beautiful. From the way everyone was groping each other and making out on the dance floor, I felt like I'd walked into some kind of prelim to an orgy. It gave me the chills.

"What have we here, Celeste?" smiled another bouncer with long, red hair and a multitude of piercings lining his eyebrows. "Fresh meat?"

Celeste threw her head back and laughed. "You wish. No, we're going downstairs."

His eyebrows shot up. "With her?"

"Yes," she replied, grabbing my hand and pulling me away. "We're expected."

As we moved towards the other side of the club, I tried not to gawk at the couples. Many of them had their hands under each other's clothing, some were even partially naked.

"Is that legal?" I asked, noticing a girl sitting on a handsome guy's lap. She was wearing a short, loose skirt and I could tell from the way she was moving her hips and moaning that they were having sex right out in the open. Before I could tear my eyes away, I met her lover's gaze and there was a flash of feral vampire lust glowing brightly.

"Legal? Probably not, but I won't tell if you won't," teased Celeste.

Embarrassed to be caught looking, I looked away from the couple and kept moving.

As we continued through the club, I noticed right away that they weren't the only couple having sex. Some of them were doing it so blatantly that I felt dirty just being near them.

"This is nuts," I whispered, lowering my eyes until I could only see the floor. Watching the other couples doing their deeds out in the open made me feel like I needed to go directly to church and confess *their* sins. As far as I was concerned, the place was creepy and I'd never be back, especially after hours.

"We're taking the elevator," said Celeste as we moved to another hallway.

"Okay," I said, following her. Soon we came upon a single mirrored elevator and she pushed the button to go down.

"So, what do you think?" she asked as we waited.

"The club? I guess it's not really my thing."

"Does it make you uncomfortable?" she asked as we got into the elevator.

I sighed. "If you ask me, it's disgusting."

"Duncan didn't seem to think so. He's always been a very willing participant," she said, her eyes beginning to glow.

I frowned. "Did… did *you* have sex with him, here?"

"Do you really want to know?" she asked, with a wicked smile.

No, I didn't.

I looked away and was silent as we took the elevator down several floors. When we reached the bottom, the door opened up into another long hallway.

"Where are we going?" I asked, following her.

"It's a surprise," she said.

"I don't think I can handle any more of those. Where's Ethan?"

"Don't worry, you'll see him soon enough."

Something in the way she said that made me hesitate.

"Celeste," I asked. "Why didn't Ethan come back for me himself?"

She stopped and turned to me. "He was very busy."

"I… I just don't understand."

She grabbed my hand. "Just, come with me if you want to see him."

I sighed and let her drag me to the end of the hallway, to a large double-doorway, where I could hear loud music coming from the other side.

As she opened it and we took our first steps, my eyes strained to adjust to the darkness inside.

"My my..." giggled Celeste, "Now what is going on over there?"

I turned my head to look and noticed we'd happened upon another creepy sex scene, this one a *ménage à trois*. I didn't recognize the two girls, who were both dressed in leather and chainmail, but as my eyes began to adjust to the low lighting, I did recognize the guy lying on the bed.

"Uh, oh," chuckled Celeste.

"Ethan?" I choked, unable to believe my eyes.

Ethan's head shot up from the center of the bed and our eyes met. "Nikki?"

I turned around and ran out of the room towards the elevators, which were thankfully, still in the basement. I slipped inside, pressed the "close" button, and began sobbing.

Chapter Twenty-four

I was still crying when I left the front doors of the club. Trevor had tried to talk to me, but I'd ignored him and walked away, wanting to escape the memory of seeing Ethan entwined between those two girls.

"Need a ride?" asked a young couple who appeared to be getting ready to leave the nightclub. From the way the guy was ogling me, I knew his ride meant something totally different than mine, and from what I'd witnessed in the club, it didn't surprise me.

Willing myself to be brave, I turned away from them and wiped the tears from my face. "No, thanks."

"It's dangerous to be wandering the streets like this," called his girlfriend from the passenger side. "Are you sure?"

"No, thanks. I'll be fine," I said as I kept walking towards Main Street.

Duncan's house wasn't too far and although it was early morning, I decided to see if he'd made it home. As I neared his house, I realized in relief that their kitchen lights were on. I hurried to the door and knocked.

The door opened and I sighed in relief. "Duncan?"

His face broke into a wide, relieved grin.

"Nikki. Thank God," he said, pulling me into the house. "We've been looking for you all night. Your mom is even here."

"Nikki!" cried my mother, rushing towards me. She threw her arms around my shoulders and pulled me close. "Thank God you're alive! I was so worried about you!"

"I'm fine," I murmured as she released me and stared into my face.

"You sure?" asked Sonny, moving towards me. "Those vampires didn't get you?"

I stared at Sonny in shock. "You know about the vampires?"

He nodded. "I've known about them for a while now. Duncan just confirmed everything tonight, however."

"Seriously, you really knew?"

Sonny sighed. "I had a suspicion. Especially after those girls started dying, and your old neighbor, Abigail, paid me a visit last summer. After she was murdered, I knew she'd been on to something. It was just hard to swallow at the time. Vampires are supposed to be fictional characters, not members of the city council."

I turned to Duncan, who looked pale but didn't have any bruises or cuts. "Are you okay?"

"I'm fine, I heal pretty quickly. By the way, where is that asshole?" he asked.

I lowered my eyes. "He's at the club."

His eyes narrowed. "Nightshade?" he asked. "Were you there, too?"

"Yeah, but not for very long. Um...where's Nathan?" I asked, looking around.

"He's searching around town for you with Caleb," said mom. "I'd better let them know. Listen, Nikki, I want you to know, Duncan and Sonny finally convinced me," she said, smiling weakly. "I'm so sorry I didn't believe you. I feel like such a horrible mother."

I gave her a hug. "It's okay, mom. I'm just glad you're safe and that you know."

"Of course I'm safe," she said, pulling away to look into my eyes. "Caleb's been watching over me."

I raised my eyebrows. "You do realize he's a vampire, too, right?"

She let out a ragged sigh. "Yes, I know. I still love him though, Nikki. I can't help it."

I understood it more than she realized. I was still in love with Ethan, even though he'd grabbed my heart, taken a bite, and then spit it out. More than once, obviously.

"You're not going to let him turn you into one of those things, are you?" I asked, staring into her eyes, which weren't covered with sunglasses for once.

She bit the side of her lip. "He says that I have cancer."

"Mom, you don't know for sure."

"I guess I'll have to find out for certain then," she said, looking away.

"Listen," said Sonny. "Caleb's a pretty decent guy and all, but the truth of the matter is... these guys feed on us."

"Some of them can't help it." My eyes met Duncan's and he smiled sheepishly.

Sonny noticed our exchange. "Shit, you know I love you, Dunc," said Sonny, patting him on the back. "And I will do anything to help you overcome this... blood thirst thing of yours. But the hell if I'm going to stand back and let the rest of those monsters kill any more folks in town."

"Sonny, they're not all monsters," said my mom.

"Anne," he replied. "I know how you feel about Caleb, but the truth of the matter is, he's behind most of these murders. I mean, listen, he's probably the head of their group. You have to stay away from him and keep your family safe. It's too dangerous for any human to associate with the likes of them. Look at what happened to Nikki tonight. What if she would have turned up dead?"

My mom closed her eyes and nodded. "I know you're right. I'd never forgive myself."

"We have to stick together," said Sonny. "And beat these creatures. Maybe get more people involved. Shit, maybe we can run them out of town."

"There's one more thing," I said. "Faye Dunbar."

Sonny's eyes narrowed. "Who is she?"

Duncan's face darkened. "She's pure evil, that's what she is."

"They say she's some kind of shape-shifter," I said.

Sonny smirked. "Shape-shifter? Christ. Well, we'll have to take care of her, too then, I guess."

"Something tells me it won't be that easy," I said.

"None of it is going to be easy," said Sonny. "But we have to try."

***

When my brother and Caleb returned, my mother didn't say much. I could tell she was confused and mulling things over in her mind.

"Thank goodness, you're all right," said Caleb, looking genuinely relieved to see me.

"Didn't Celeste call and tell you she found me?" I asked him.

"I haven't spoken to her all night," he replied.

"Really? Well, she picked me up in your new car; I just figured you would have known."

He raised his eyebrows. "New car?"

"A Mercedes?" I answered. "She picked me up in it around three this morning."

"I'll bet its Drake's new car," he said. "I only have my Cherokee and the squad car."

"Well, maybe I just misunderstood her," I said.

The truth of the matter was, I didn't understand anything that happened after she'd picked me up. The entire time I'd been with her, she'd seemed more secretive than usual and appeared almost giddy when I'd found Ethan with the two girls.

"Maybe. I'm just glad you're back with your family," said Caleb.

"How did Celeste find you?" asked Nathan.

"It's a long story," I mumbled. I wasn't even sure what had happened myself.

"I told Caleb about the girl you found earlier," said Nathan.

"Yeah, we're looking into it," said Caleb.

"It was Faye Dunbar," I said. "You need to investigate her."

"She has an alibi," said Caleb. "I already questioned her."

Of course.

My mom yawned. "We should get back to the cabin. It's very late and we could all use the rest."

"What about you, sweetheart? You doing okay?" Caleb asked, rubbing my mom's shoulders.

"I um...I'm fine," she murmured.

His eyes narrowed. "Do we need to talk?"

"It is really late," I interrupted. "We should get back to the cabin, mom."

"I'll drive you guys back," said Caleb."

"No," I said, "Sonny's already volunteered."

Caleb turned to Sonny. "You sure?"

Sonny nodded. "It's no problem at all. I've been meaning to check out their boat anyway. Make sure Nathan winterized it properly."

"Okay, well thanks, Sonny. Listen, hon," said Caleb, turning back towards my mother. "I've got to go and look for that Ethan character. You make sure you get some sleep. I want you raring to go when it comes time to catch our plane tomorrow morning. Okay?"

"Of course," she said, not meeting his eyes as he studied her.

"Caleb, if you're looking for Ethan, he was at Club Nightshade the last time I looked," I said.

"Okay, thanks," he replied. "Listen, Nikki, you have to say away from Ethan," he said. "That kid is bad news. When I get my hands on him, he's in deep shit. Are you sure you don't want to press kidnapping charges?"

I shook my head and could tell he was relieved.

"Okay, then," he said, "But, if you change your mind, just let me know."

"Sure," I said.

After Caleb left, Sonny released a long breath. "Now that I know what he really is, it scares the hell out of me."

"I had to drive around with him," complained Nathan. "Every time he looked at me, I wondered if I was a goner."

Duncan sighed. "Caleb's not going to attack you. He definitely wants your mom and isn't going to do anything that might jeopardize that relationship."

"Oh, God…what am I going to do?" moaned my mom, sitting down on a chair. "He still expects me to go."

"You need to get out of town," said Sonny. "You can't stay in Shore Lake anymore. In fact, it's not safe for you or Nikki. I'm going to make some calls and see if I can find a safe place for you."

"Okay," she answered, nodding. "I'd appreciate any help you can give us."

From the look on my mom's face, I could tell she was more than a little distraught. I grabbed her hand. "Mom, it's going to work out."

She nodded in agreement but still looked pensive.

"Duncan? You okay?" asked Nathan.

I turned to stare at Duncan, who appeared to be sweating and shaky.

"I'm fine," he murmured, clenching and unclenching his fist.

From the way he was acting, I knew exactly what was wrong with him. "You need to feed," I said.

"I'll be fine," said Duncan, stumbling towards the hallway leading towards the bathroom.

I followed him. "Duncan?"

He closed the door and locked it.

I knocked. "Duncan?"

"Leave me alone," he answered.

"What's going on?" asked Sonny, standing next to me.

"He has to feed," I said.

Sonny pounded on the door. "Son? You okay?"

I could hear Duncan groaning in the bathroom. "I'm fine, just leave me alone," he said.

"What can I do for you?" asked Sonny. "Just tell me."

"Just leave me be," growled Duncan.

"I'll give him some blood," I whispered. "It will help him."

Sonny shook his head and began rolling up his sleeve. "The hell you will. If anyone is going to volunteer, it will be me. I'm his father and I've got a lot more to spare then you, honey."

"Go away," demanded Duncan. "I won't take it from either of you."

"Duncan," I pleaded. "You need to feed."

The door suddenly opened and Duncan stood staring at us, swaying slightly. "Excuse me."

We moved out of the way, and before either of us could blink, Duncan was gone and we could hear the front door slam.

"Jesus," said Sonny. "How the hell can he move that fast?"

"He's no longer human," I said, closing my eyes.

Chapter Twenty-five

Sonny packed everyone into his Tahoe and proceeded to take us home around five-thirty that morning. My mom sat in front with him while Nathan and I rode in the back.

"I hope Duncan will be okay," said Sonny, rubbing his chin. "I feel so damn helpless. I can't do anything for him except give him my support. It's frustrating."

"He'll be okay," said mom. "Duncan's a smart kid and I know he'll do the right thing."

"He's also not like the rest of them," I said. "He'd never take it from someone by force. In fact, he probably went to Nightshade; apparently they have very willing donors."

"It's barbaric," whispered my mom. "The more I think about it, the more it disturbs me."

"You have no idea what barbaric is," I said, "Until you've walked into that sick place."

I then told them about the things I'd seen in the club, leaving out the part of walking in on Ethan having sex. It was still too painful to talk about.

"The club isn't always like that," said Nathan."

Mom turned around. "How would you know?"

He shrugged. "Celeste took me there before."

She scowled. "I wasn't aware of that."

"You've been too busy with Caleb," I mumbled.

She sighed but didn't say anything.

"I'm exhausted," yawned Nathan. "I could sleep for days."

Before long, we were back at the cabin and memories of what happened earlier came to mind.

"Great," I mumbled, walking up the stairs towards my room. "Duncan and Ethan were in my bedroom earlier. I don't even want to see the damage."

"What?" asked mom.

"They were fighting over Nikki," said Nathan.

Mom followed me to my bedroom and we both groaned in horror at the horrible mess. My bed was in shambles, my pictures and everything was knocked down from my dresser, and there was broken glass on the carpet.

"How in the world did they get blood on the ceiling?" cringed my mother.

"Don't ask," I said, picking up broken pieces of my alarm clock.

"This is going to take a long time to clean," she said. "Why don't you just sleep in my room for now?"

I nodded. "Okay. I'm too tired to deal with this mess now anyway."

"I'll be joining you in a few," she said. "I'll see Sonny out and then be back up."

I changed into a clean T-shirt and shorts then shuffled into her room, exhausted. As I lay in my mom's bed, I thought about Ethan and how he'd lied to me about everything. Nothing he'd done had made sense, and when I finally fell asleep, my dreams were troubled.

A half hour later, I woke up to the sounds of screams.

"No!" screamed my mother from somewhere down below.

I leaped out of bed and rushed down the steps. When I made it to the main floor, I noticed she was nowhere to be found but the front door was wide open.

"What's going on?" hollered Nathan, coming up behind me.

"It's mom," I said. "She was screaming."

He bolted around me and I followed him outside.

"Mom!" he yelled.

We stepped off of the porch and walked around the deck, towards the lake. It was then that we both froze in shock.

"Sonny!" screamed Nathan in anguish.

"Oh, my God!" I choked.

Sonny's body lay broken and twisted near the boat launch, his eyes staring blindly up into the early morning light. We ran to his body and crouched down, trying to find a pulse.

"Who could have done this?" I cried.

Nathan scowled. "Probably Ethan or Caleb."

I stared at him in horror. "Or Faye?"

He didn't say anything.

"Nathan, where's mom?" I whispered, looking around.

He stood up and wiped the tears from his face. "Mom!"

"Mom!" I yelled, getting back to my feet. "Mom!"

We started walking back towards the house, calling frantically for her, but she didn't answer.

"I just heard her screaming!" I cried. "She can't be too far."

"Caleb must have taken her. We have to go and search for her."

I nodded. "I think he knew something was wrong when he brought you back to Sonny's."

"Let's go back into the house and get dressed. We'll need some weapons or something. Shit!" he hollered, frantically running a hand through his hair. "What the hell can we even use against these things?"

I was already running up the stairs. "I don't know, but let's find something sharp!"

I quickly got dressed and then went back downstairs, where I grabbed a butcher knife from the kitchen.

"We need Duncan," said Nathan, coming up behind me. He grabbed his cell phone from the counter and tried calling his number.

"He's going to be wrecked," I moaned, thinking about how much he loved his father. "Poor Duncan."

Nathan closed his eyes and nodded. "Come on," he said into the phone. "Pick up, bro."

When Duncan didn't answer, Nathan slammed his phone down on the counter.

"Don't! You'll break it and then she won't be able to contact you."

He picked it back up and reached for his own knife from the butcher block. Then we drove back to Duncan's house and as I kind of expected, he wasn't home.

"Should we check the club?" I asked nervously, although the last thing in the world I wanted to see was him with another girl, even if he was just feeding.

"We don't have time," said Nathan. "Let's go get mom before Caleb does something disgusting and irreversible to her."

I nodded in agreement.

When we arrived at Caleb's mansion, it was eerily quiet.

"Well, Caleb's squad car is here," said Nathan, gripping his knife firmly. "And there," he pointed, "is his Jeep."

I noticed there were two other cars parked in front of the house, but I didn't recognize either of them.

"Should we knock?" I whispered as we stepped onto the porch, both weapons in hand. I really didn't think we'd have much chance with the weapons, but it gave me extra courage.

He licked his lips and shook his head. "No, let's just go in. Chances are they know we're here anyway."

My heart was pounding as he turned the knob and I half expected Celeste to greet us like she did the day before, this time, however, as an enemy. Fortunately, I was wrong.

"What are we going to do if he won't let us see her?" I whispered.

"He has to. I won't take no for an answer," snapped Nathan.

We searched the lower level first, but found no signs of anyone.

"I'm sure they're upstairs," he whispered. "Resting or whatever it is they do."

I nodded and followed him. As we crept upstairs, I could hear myself breathing heavily with fear.

Suddenly Nathan stopped and I slammed into him. "Listen," he whispered, turning to glance at me. "If this doesn't go the way we'd planned, I just want to say sorry for doubting you these past few months, and...I love you, Twerp."

"Me too," I whispered.

He released a shaky sigh. "I hope this plan works and we don't end up as bat food."

"Nathan, I don't think these particular vampires turn into bats."

"Whatever. Let's just have each other's backs at all costs."

I nodded and continued to follow him.

After inspecting three bedrooms on the second level and finding nothing, we went up to the third and final level.

"I've been up here before. This is where Ethan's room was."

"I hope he's back so I can slice his throat," mumbled Nathan.

We proceeded to check each of the bedrooms and found they were also empty.

"What's going on?" I whispered angrily. "Where the hell is everyone?"

He sucked on his lower lip for a while and then his eyes lit up. "You know what? Let's check the cellar. I mean, shit, they must have one of those? Don't vampires like dark, dank places?"

I shrugged. "Honestly, I don't know. These vampires are different than the others."

He raised his eyebrows. "Others? You mean they're different than what...the fictional ones?"

I smiled sheepishly. "Yeah, that's what I meant."

He snickered and began walking away. I quickly followed.

We went back down the steps and next to the kitchen, we eventually found another set leading to the cellar. As we began to descend the rickety staircase, I heard an unearthly growl from somewhere down below.

"Did you hear that?" I squeaked, pausing on the steps.

He nodded. "Sounds like some kind of animal."

"I don't think we should go down there," I whispered, my eyes straining to see down into the darkness.

He sighed. "I don't either, but we have no choice. I mean, what if mom's down here?"

I bit the side of my lip and nodded. "Okay. Yeah, fine. Let's go before I change my mind."

Every step creaked against our weight, making it all much more ominous.

"We should have brought a flashlight," I told him, trying not to fall.

"We weren't exactly planning this to begin with," replied Nathan.

There was another growl, followed by a pained moan.

"Oh, crap, Nathan!" I whispered loudly. "This is nuts. We're going to get ourselves killed!"

He raised his hand. "Shush."

The cellar was large and filled with old boxes and jars of things I didn't even want to know about.

"Look," he pointed when he reached the bottom first.

On the other side of the basement or cellar, whatever the hell it was, we saw a single door with a light shining underneath. As we stared at it, another moan escaped from the other side, one that made the hair stand up on the back of my neck.

"Stay behind me," whispered Nathan.

We stepped quietly towards the closed door until we were just outside. When Nathan put his hand on the knob, I had another panic attack.

"No," I whispered, on the verge of hysteria. "We should think about this. We don't know who or what is in there."

"We don't have any other choice," he whispered. "Every second that ticks brings mom closer to an eternity spent as a blood hunter. Look, if you're too chicken, I'll just go in myself."

"I'm not chicken," I snapped, secretly praying that the door was locked.

"Right," he whispered, turning the knob. When he started pulling the door open, my chest tightened up, making it hard to breathe.

Crap.

I did not want to know what was on the other side of that door, but of course it was already too late. Nathan swung it open and both of us froze in horror at what was waiting on the other side.

Chapter Twenty-six

"What is it?" I squeaked, unable to stop gawking at the hideous creature sitting with its back against the wall. Thankfully, it was caged in some kind of makeshift prison and there were thick metal bars separating us.

"Jesus," shuddered Nathan. "I have no fucking clue."

It was very thin and wore a pair of dark jeans that seemed to hang from its bony hips. I stared at its gaunt face, which looked shrunken and withered past the point of being alive. When it opened its eyes, I felt as if the air was sucked right out of me.

"Oh, God!" I choked, recognizing the crystal blue eyes. "Ethan?"

His lips curled up into a grim smile and then his head fell forward as if he'd expended the last of his energy.

I rushed to the cell and tried desperately to open it. When that didn't work, I began to shake it in frustration.

"What the hell are you doing?" barked Nathan, trying to pull me away.

"It's Ethan!" I cried. "We have to help him!"

Nathan turned towards Ethan and scowled. "If it really is that asshole, why should we help him after everything that's happened?"

I didn't care what he'd done at that point. My heart cried out and I wanted nothing more than to save him. "He needs us! Please, we have to help him."

Nathan raised his hands in exasperation and moved away from me. "I'm not helping him. In fact, I think he's well beyond help. I mean, look at him!"

I turned to look at Ethan and it broke my heart. It looked as if someone had sucked the life right out of him, either a vampire or something far worse. Then it hit me...

"Faye," I whispered.

Ethan opened his eyes, again and blinked quickly, as if trying to answer my question.

I reached an arm through the bars. "Ethan," I cried. "Come here, let me help you!"

Ethan shook his head and closed his eyes.

"Are you fucking crazy!" hollered Nathan, pulling me back away from the cell again. "What in the hell are you thinking?"

"He needs me," I sobbed. "He'll die if we don't do something."

"So let him," snapped Nathan. "You can't save him, and from what I can see, he needs more than just a little blood to bring his skinny ass back. It would probably kill you to even try."

"He's right," murmured a smooth voice behind us.

We both turned to see Drake standing in the doorway, staring at us with his now-familiar cocky, disarming smile.

"Stay the fuck away from us, vampire," snapped Nathan, raising his knife.

Drake sighed in and then walked around Nathan towards the prison cell. "You have nothing to fear from me, mate. I'm here to help Ethan."

"Yeah, right," said Nathan. "It's kind of a coincidence that you showed up here the same time as us."

"I just finished having breakfast," he replied with a dark smile. "Which is lucky for Ethan, as well as you."

"Can you save him?" I asked, wiping the tears from my face.

Drake tore off the lock without breaking a sweat. "I'm going to bloody well try. This bloke and

I have been friends for far too long to just let him dry up into a pile of dust."

Ethan opened his eyes and I saw a flicker of amusement in them.

Drake crouched down next to Ethan and laughed. "Looking pretty rough, mate; not a good look for a randy vampire such as yourself I must say. Remind me to never get on Faye's bad side. Now, smile and show me some teeth."

Ethan opened his mouth and Drake offered him his wrist.

"You're just lucky I'm such a good friend. Now, remember to go slow or I'll have to kick your bloomin' ass," he said as Ethan closed his eyes and began to feed.

Nathan and I watched in stunned silence as Ethan slowly began to change. First his cheeks began to fill out, then his legs and arms; finally his chest and muscles began to take on the shape I'd remembered. When it was over, he lay breathless and pale, as did Drake.

"Have to refuel," groaned Drake, as he struggled to get up. He actually looked like he was ready to pass out himself. "Anyone care to volunteer?"

"I don't think so, pal," snapped my brother. "I didn't sign up to be on anyone's menu now or in the future."

"Such a delightful character," breathed Drake.

"Drake, are you going to be okay?" I asked him.

He staggered over to me and then steadied himself using the wall. "You know," he murmured, staring down at me. "If Ethan wasn't so smitten by you," he teased, "I'd take you away from all of this and make you forget about that bloke."

I could tell by the look in his eyes he wasn't lying, either. My cheeks turned pink.

"I hope we meet again, under better circumstances," he said, grabbing my hand. His was so cool, it gave me goose bumps.

"I agree," I said as he kissed my knuckles.

"You saved my life, friend, but that means we're even and I no longer owe you," said Ethan, coming up behind me. He slipped his arms around my waist and pulled me back against his body.

"He's not very good at saying 'thank you'," chuckled Drake with a gleam in his eyes. "Is he?"

I opened my mouth but couldn't respond because I was so flustered, especially now that Ethan seemed to be claiming me once again.

Ethan reached out a hand and gave him a slight shove. "Thanks. Now go and feed before you make yourself more dangerous around Nikki than you already are."

"You know me all too well," said Drake. "Take care of this little lady and stay away from the shape-shifter. Didn't I warn you about her before?"

"Yes, I should have listened."

Drake turned to my brother and chuckled. "Nice seeing you again, Nate. I hope you get over your attitude. Not all of us are the monsters you may think we are."

My brother glared at him. "It's Nathan."

"Nathan," he said and turned back to me. "Nikki, you've got your hands full with these two blokes," said Drake. "You sure you don't want to come with me? I'll be heading back to New York soon. You'd be like... a breath of fresh air."

Before I could respond, Ethan cut in. "Goodbye, Drake," he said.

Drake laughed and turned to leave. "Try to stay out of trouble, all of you."

"Easier said than done," mumbled Ethan.

I stepped out of Ethan's grasp as soon as Drake left and turned on him, my confusion now replaced with anger. "What in the hell is up with you?"

He stared at me in confusion. "What?"

Nathan, sensing I was about to explode, backed away towards the door. "I'll meet you upstairs, Nikk, and you... Fangs," he said to Ethan. "You hurt my sister, in any way, I'll skin you alive."

Ethan shook his head in exasperation.

"I'll be right up, Nathan," I said.

"Now, tell me what's wrong?" asked Ethan once we were alone.

I scowled. "What's wrong? Do you even have to ask?"

He sighed and ran a hand through his dark hair. "I've had a rough night and don't have time for games. What exactly are you referring to this time?"

I tapped my foot on the ground, angrily. "Yeah, I know you had a rough night, lover boy. Before you were turned into a...a... mummy, you were worked over by a couple of girls. You don't recall that?"

His eyebrows shot up. "What?"

I folded my arms under my chest and leaned forward. "Oh, you don't remember that part of your adventure?"

He smiled. "Wait a second, where and when did this happen? And I was with two girls, you say?"

"You were at Club Nightshade," I snapped. "Just a few hours ago."

He chuckled. "Listen, you may have been there, but I certainly wasn't."

"That's crap. Celeste picked me up at the cabin, brought me to the club, and there you were, getting it on with two dominatrix-type of skanks."

He laughed. "Are you serious? Did they whip me?"

I glared at him. "Not funny."

He sighed and then grabbed my shoulders. "Listen to me, I swear to God," he said, staring into my eyes. "I wasn't there. I left you at the cabin and came straight here, like I said I would. Unfortunately, Faye was also here and like an idiot, I walked into some kind of trap. The next thing I knew, I was locked inside of that cell, unable to move because she'd somehow drained me of both my blood and energy."

"Why would she do that? I thought you were her little 'boy toy'?"

He frowned. "Who said that?"

"Celeste."

He dropped his arms and ran a hand over his face. "Okay, fine...we had something a long time ago but it was clearly a mistake. Once I found out how dangerous and twisted Faye was, it drove me away. The only reason I was at the diner with her yesterday was because I knew she was up to something and I wanted to find out exactly what. Then, when you stopped over to our table, I could actually feel her rage. That's the only reason I blew you off. She'd have killed you if she knew my true feelings."

"Well, I felt her true feelings about me. In fact sometimes I can hear her in my head."

"You can?" He frowned. "She was probably toying with you. She can connect to anyone she wants and send them messages."

I raised my eyebrows. "Why in the world would she do that?"

"Like I said before, she's twisted and crazy. I guess you could say that she likes to play with her food before she eats it."

My jaw dropped. "Are you saying I'm on her menu?"

"I'm saying that you definitely still need my protection, because she's obviously after you."

"Oh really? Well, you didn't do so well protecting yourself," I said.

His face darkened. "I wasn't prepared before; this time I am."

The image of him with the two girls flashed through my mind, again. "I still don't understand who was at the club earlier, if it wasn't you."

He shrugged. "I'm sure it was Faye."

I didn't expect that answer. "What?"

"As I've been trying to tell you, she's a shape-shifter. She can transform into anyone she wants. Obviously, she had Celeste helping her out this time."

"Celeste?"

"Celeste would do anything for Faye. She idolizes her."

"This is all so confusing," I mumbled, feeling slightly dizzy.

He grabbed me and pulled me into his arms. "The only thing you have to remember is that I love you and there is nobody else," he murmured into my hair.

"What about Miranda?" I whispered, catching a trace of his butterscotch scent.

He stiffened up.

"Ethan?"

Sighing, he pulled away and raised my chin. "I love you, Nikki. I realize that you're not Miranda, nor do I want you to be."

"That's a relief," I murmured.

"Now, although I'd love nothing more than to take you up to my bedroom and have my way with you, it's much too dangerous here."

"Which reminds me," I said. "Where do you think Caleb took my mother?"

His eyebrows shot up. "Your mother is missing?"

"Yes. I'm sure Caleb took her. He also murdered Sonny, Duncan's dad."

"What about Duncan? Did he get him?"

I pushed him. "This isn't a joke. My mom is missing and Sonny's dead! He was a nice man and Duncan doesn't deserve any of this!"

He grabbed me and held me to him. "Calm down. I'll help you find your mom."

"Thank you," I answered, into his chest. "Now, let's go."

He followed me upstairs to the kitchen.

"Huh, Nathan must be outside waiting," I said as we moved through the house.

"Let me check the rest of the house first," said Ethan, disappearing.

Two seconds later he returned wearing a dark pair of sunglasses and new clothes. "He's definitely not inside. Good news is, I found my other pair of sunglasses."

"I'm thrilled for you," I mumbled, opening the front door. I walked outside and stared at the Mustang, which was empty. "What the hell?"

"Nathan!" yelled Ethan, his booming voice louder than I could have possibly imagined.

"Ethan," I winced, covering my ears.

He walked towards the Mustang and bent down. "There's been a scuffle," he said, pointing towards the dirt.

I looked down towards the ground; sure enough, someone had either been dancing or struggling with someone else.

"Crap," I said. "Where do you think he is?

He shrugged. "The club?"

I raised my eyebrows. "The club? Why in the world would he be there?" I asked.

"Something tells me that Faye has him. She owns Club Nightshade."

Chapter Twenty-seven

"You're not coming," argued Ethan. "It's too dangerous."

"Well, you're definitely not going alone. You didn't fare too well last time all by yourself," I said. "Besides, aren't you still pretty weak?"

"I'm fine."

"Ethan, if you need blood..."

"Are you offering?"

I swallowed. "Only, if it's going to help save Nathan."

He smiled seductively and touched my stomach. "Right now, blood isn't what I'm craving."

I ignored him. "As I was saying....I'm going with you, like it or not."

He blew out an exasperated breath. "Don't you see? It's what she wants. She's using your brother as bait."

I scowled. "I don't care. You have to let me go with you. How do we know that she isn't trying to separate us? I'd be even more vulnerable if you left me alone. Maybe that's her plan."

Ethan sighed. "Good point."

"Damn right it is."

"Fine," he grumbled, finally relenting. "You can come, but that means you do exactly what I say."

Okay," I said.

His eyes narrowed. "Exactly, Nikki."

"I said I will."

He nodded. "Okay, start by removing your clothes."

My eyes widened. "What?"

There was a twinkle in his eyes. "See, you're already questioning my orders."

"Ethan," I warned, biting back a smile.

He smirked. "I had to try."

"We're wasting time."

"Okay then, let's go," he said, moving towards me.

"Whoa...how about we drive this time?" I said, taking a step back.

"That takes much too long," he said, pulling me into his arms. "Like you said, we're already wasting time."

I held my breath as he launched into the air. Seconds later, we were behind the club and I was fighting another wave of nausea.

"You okay?" he asked, looking down at me.

"Just a little dizzy," I mumbled, pulling away. The last thing I wanted to do was puke in his arms.

"Don't worry, Nikki. You'll get used to it."

"Right," I said.

"Well," he said, trying to open one of the delivery doors.

"I thought you were really powerful. Can't you just rip the door off?"

"There's probably and alarm on these doors. It would give us away."

"Oh, yeah."

"Obviously it's closed, and we can't just enter through the front, either. She's probably monitoring the entrance."

"What do you recommend?"

He looked up. "We should try the roof. Ready?"

I backed away from him as he advanced towards me.

"Why don't you come back down and let me in through one of these doors?"

He shook his head. "I'm not leaving you alone. This was your idea, remember?"

"Fine, let's go."

As it turned out, there was a penthouse on the roof.

"This is where Faye stays when she's in town," he said. "I haven't been up here yet, but she told me a little about it."

"Right," I mumbled.

He grinned. "I haven't. Seriously."

"How can you enter her place if you haven't been invited in?"

"But I have been invited, Nikki. I never said I hadn't."

"Oh."

I followed Ethan through a sliding glass door that led to a wide, open living room which was more luxurious than anything I'd ever encountered.

"This place is amazing," I said.

The walls were covered with different types of artwork that probably cost more than my mother's annual salary, and the contemporary leather furniture sitting next to white fireplace reminded me of something I'd recently seen in some magazine.

"She lives pretty lavishly," said Ethan, motioning towards the white piano sitting in the corner of the room.

"I guess," I murmured.

"At least she isn't here," he said. "I can't smell her."

I raised my eyebrows. "You could smell her?"

"Our senses are superior to those of humans. It's what makes us good hunters."

"Oh," I shuddered.

He bit back a smile. "Let's go."

We left the penthouse and made our way down the emergency stairwell. When we reached the bottom, he looked at me. "Stay behind and don't say anything. I'm going to try and reason with Faye."

"Will that work?"

He frowned. "Probably not."

He opened the door and we stepped into a long hallway near the same elevator I'd taken to the lower level.

"Ethan, I'll bet they're in the basement."

"Maybe, but as long as we're here, let's check the main club area first."

I nodded and followed his lead.

Most of the lights were out in the club as we snuck inside, but there were a couple of employees cleaning the bar and stocking the shelves with more booze.

"I don't see any sign of your brother, nor do I smell his bullshit," he whispered as we crouched down behind one of the walls separating the large dance floor.

I elbowed him. "Very funny."

He bit back a smile. "I guess that leaves the basement."

"What if he's not here?"

"We'll go back to your cabin then. Maybe that's where they're holding him, waiting for you to show up."

"What about my mom? Caleb talked about bringing her to Vegas tomorrow."

He frowned. "Faye owns a hotel in Vegas. I'll bet he's taken your mom there."

"Do you know where it is?" I whispered.

He nodded. "I can show you."

"Thanks, Ethan."

We ducked out of the bar and made our way to the elevators, but didn't see any kind of stairwell leading down to the basement.

"They must have an emergency exit somewhere else," he said. "I don't know if I want to take the elevator and announce our presence."

"But it might be the only way to save Nathan."

He nodded. "I know. We have to find another way, though. I'm not risking you getting hurt."

Just then, the elevator lights were blinking. Ethan grabbed me and whisked us away back into the club, where we ducked down under some tables. Seconds later, Faye walked into the club with a large bald guy wearing a suit. He reminded me of a gangster.

"I need a drink," declared Faye, moving behind the bar.

The barrel-chested man said nothing, only sat down across from her at the bar.

"So, Lucas, what have you done with the boy?" she asked.

He cleared his throat. "We took him back to the cabin to wait for his sister."

She filled herself a shot glass full of whiskey and slammed it. "Good," she replied breathlessly, refilling it again. "I'm sure they'll head back that way. What about the other kid?"

"He's on his way, I'm sure. I told him you'd help his...cause."

"Ah... I'm sure he's pissed. What about Caleb? Did he leave town?" she asked.

"I believe so."

She sighed. "I can't believe he's so gung-ho about that human. If I didn't need Caleb, I'd kill them both."

"Caleb has definitely become a loose cannon," said the bald guy. "He's going to put us all at risk with his actions. If I may make a suggestion?"

"Certainly," she replied.

"You should consider getting rid of that entire clan of Roamers. You know, there's going to be a deep investigation with all of the recent murders. It might put some heat on you and that would be bad for business."

"You're probably right. It would be a pity to kill Celeste; however, she's been so useful."

He sighed. "You'd have no choice. She'd seek revenge if you killed her father, Faye."

Faye nodded. "Very well, do it quickly."

My breath caught in my throat.

Ethan put a finger over his lips as warning.

The bald man's cell phone went off and he answered it.

"The kid is here," he said after he hung up.

"Good," replied Faye.

Seconds later we watched in shock as Duncan was ushered into the bar.

"Duncan," smiled Faye, holding out her hand. "Very nice to meet you."

"Where is he?" growled Duncan, ignoring the friendly gesture.

Faye stared at him for a second and then sighed. "We aren't sure. He's escaped."

Duncan's fists were clenched. "I'm going to kill him."

I turned to Ethan, whose expression was unreadable."

"Did you see him do it?" asked Duncan. "Did you see him kill my father?"

Faye nodded. "Yes, it was him. I saw it with my own eyes. He killed your father, broke his neck without a second thought. All for that... girl," she snarled.

"But, you saw him do it?"

She touched his arm. "Yes, I'm sorry and want to help you. We all know that Ethan is a coldblooded murderer and needs to be stopped once and for all."

"So, you'll really help me find him?"

A slow smiled spread over Faye's lips. "Oh, yes. I'll help you if you help me."

Duncan frowned. "What do you want from me?"

"Nikki. I want her."

Duncan's lips thinned. "Why?"

Faye tapped her nails on the bar. "Because," she sighed, "Nikki is Miranda."

"What do you mean by that?" he asked.

Before she could answer, Ethan grabbed my arm and pulled me out of the bar.

"We have to go," he whispered.

I stopped walking. "Why did she call me Miranda?" I said. "This is so ridiculous."

"Don't listen to her. We have to leave now. Your brother's life is in danger, as is your mom's."

"As is yours," boomed a voice behind us.

Ethan and I turned to face Duncan.

"Duncan," I said, stepping towards him.

Ethan pulled me back.

"You killed my father," growled Duncan, stepping towards us.

"No," I said, moving towards him again. "It wasn't Ethan!"

"Don't lie for him, Nikki," snapped Duncan. "He'd say or do anything to keep you interested in him."

"No, it's true," said Ethan, stepping between Duncan and myself. "I wasn't there. I've never even met your father."

"Don't listen to them," said Faye, walking up behind Duncan. She placed a hand on his shoulder. "They're both trying to trick you. Don't let them."

"You lie, Faye," snapped Ethan. "This game you're playing must end."

"Games?" said Duncan, taking another step towards us. "You know all about them. That's why Nikki is so brainwashed by your lies. I think it's time to end your games, once and for all."

I watched in shock as Duncan leaped towards Ethan and in a whirl of fists they began to fight.

"No!" I yelled, backing away.

"Grab her, Lucas!" hollered Faye, staring at me with a gleam in her eyes.

Before I could move any further, Lucas grabbed me from behind and pulled me towards the elevator, which was now opening. "Ethan!" I screamed, as I was shoved inside. The next thing I knew, Faye joined us and the elevator closed.

"Finally," sneered Faye. "I have you, Miranda."

"You're crazy!" I cried. "I'm not Miranda!"

She stepped in front of me and grabbed my chin. She stared into my eyes. "Oh, but you are. I see you in there."

"Please let me go," I begged as the elevator door opened at the top floor. "I'm, seriously not who you think I am."

"Let you go? Now, why would I want to do that?" she chuckled.

"Please, don't do this!"

They ignored my pleas and forced me into her apartment.

"Lucas, go back downstairs and shoot both of them," said Faye. "It appears we don't need Duncan now."

"Shoot them? I didn't think that would work," said Lucas.

"Shoot the Roamers in the head. It will immobilize them until I can come back down and finish the job," she said.

He nodded and left the apartment.

"Why are you doing this?" I asked.

Because it amuses me...

"You're insane," I said.

Just then something came crashing through the large plate window from the courtyard.

"Incompetent idiot," sighed Faye as Ethan stood up straight. She quickly grabbed me around the throat.

"Let her go," growled Ethan, stepping towards us slowly.

Faye's grip tightened. "Step away from us, or I'll break her neck."

He stopped. "Faye, don't do this."

"Why? Because you can't live without her?" she barked.

"Because she's just a girl. Look, she's not Miranda."

"She must die, like the rest."

He frowned. "Like the rest? What do you mean by that?"

"The bodies that Miranda has used to try and come back. I've worked very hard to stop her."

"What are you talking about?" he asked.

"She thought she could fool me, but I... I could see her in all of their eyes."

"Whose eyes?" he asked.

She laughed. "Amy, Tina, all the others. Miranda used their bodies to return to you, and now she's in Nikki's. But not for long. I'm going to find a way to stop your little bitch for good."

"You killed all of those girls?" I whispered hoarsely.

"Shut up," she growled, squeezing my throat tighter.

Just then Lucas stormed through the front door. "I got one of them," he said.

My chest grew tight. *Duncan!*

"The other one is here, now finish the job."

Ethan smirked. "You're kidding right? I'm a little faster than your bullet."

Faye pushed me to the ground. "Better yet, kill the girl instead."

There was a loud blast from the gun and then total darkness.

Chapter Twenty-eight

My dreams were a jumble of terror, grief, and hunger. When I finally woke up, there was an overwhelming need in the pit of my stomach, which ached to be satisfied.

"Ethan!" I gasped, sitting up.

I looked around and found myself alone in a strange bedroom, wearing nothing but an oversized man's button front dress shirt.

The room was cold.

I began to shiver in spite of the warm fire cracking in a nearby fireplace. I pulled the scratchy blanket in tighter to my body and stood up to get closer to the heat of the fire.

"Hey," said Ethan, walking through the door, holding a cup.

"Ethan, oh thank God," I whispered, my voice hoarse.

"Get back into bed," he said. "You're much too weak to be on your feet."

"What's happened?" I asked, sitting back down on the edge of the bed.

He put his cup down on the nightstand and sat down next to me. "You don't remember anything?" he asked, grabbing my hand.

I shook my head.

He sighed. "You've been in and out of consciousness for a few days."

"What? Where are we?"

"In the mountains of Montana," he said. "This place was deserted when I brought you here."

I licked my lips. "What's happened to my family?"

He stared into the fire. "I'm not really sure. The only thing on my mind has been you."

"Ethan, we have to go find them," I said, trying to stand on two very shaky legs.

"Wait," he said, pulling me towards his lap. "You need to rest longer. You're too weak to do anything right now."

"Then find me something to eat, so we can leave," I pleaded, feeling my stomach growl in agreement. "Please."

He pursed his lips. "There's something I have to tell you."

I scowled. "About Faye?"

"No, about you."

I stared into his eyes. "What?"

He touched my stomach. "You were shot."

I looked down where his hand was. "Shot?"

He traced a circle near my belly and I grabbed his hand. "Stop, that tickles."

"You weren't going to make it," he said, pulling me closer.

I shivered as his lips brushed the hollow of my neck. "That's ridiculous. I wasn't shot."

"Nikki," he said, lifting his face to stare into my eyes. "You were dying and I had to save you."

I narrowed my eyes. "What are you trying to say?"

He lifted me up, carried me over to a large, full-length mirror and set me down.

"What?" I asked, staring at my reflection in the mirror. I was very surprised to see his refection next to mine, since he was supposed to be some kind of vampire. Obviously, that was another misguided notion. A vampire in Shore Lake does cast a reflection.

He stood behind me and raised my chin so that my neck was exposed.

"What in the heck is that?" I whispered, shaking his hand away. I walked closer to the mirror and examined the scar.

"I had to," he murmured. "You were dying."

"You bit me?"

"We...bonded."

I turned to him. "You turned me into one of you?" I cried.

He touched my cheek. "I had no other choice. You lost too much blood."

My eyes widened. "Three times? We had sex when I was unconscious, three times?"

He smiled. "Believe me; you weren't unconscious when we made love."

"But, I don't remember. I...oh, my God," I choked. "I'm not human anymore?"

He took me into his arms. "You're alive. That's all that matters."

I stared up at him in horror. "But, do I have to drink human blood to survive now?"

He nodded. "You have to, but I guarantee, it will be much more enjoyable than you think."

I stepped away from him and shook my head. "No, I can't. There's no way I can do that."

He sighed. "You have to, or you'll die."

I started to cry. "No..."

"Nikki, it's not that bad. Once you feed, you'll be stronger and feel more alive than you've ever felt in your life. I swear to you."

"There is no way," I cried, "that I'm going to drink someone's blood."

He looked at me incredulously. "Would you rather die?"

"Maybe," I sobbed.

He frowned and pulled me into his arms. "I won't ever let that happen. I love you."

I tried to pull away but he held me firm. "Please," I begged. "Just leave me alone."

"Never," he said huskily, tightening his hold.

"Ethan," I pleaded, trying to pull away. I couldn't deal with this news now. It was bad enough that my brother and mom were missing. "Ethan, please leave me alone."

He ignored me and sought out my mouth instead. As his lips captured mine, I moaned in protest. "Stop," I breathed, as his mouth moved towards my neck. "Please."

"You'll be so much stronger," he whispered. "You can help save your family. We'll do it together."

My heart ached as images of my mother flashed through my head, along with Faye's cold, cruel stare. I closed my eyes as my body began to betray me and eventually, I gave in and met his kisses with my own.

"Ethan," I breathed against his lips, pulling him closer to me. I just wanted to forget everything but the taste and smell of his mouth and tongue mixing with mine. Quickly my kisses became more demanding, almost savage, surprising the both of us.

He groaned against my mouth and then pulled his lips away to stare into my eyes.

"Please," I whimpered, pulling him back towards me. He'd started a fire so hot I just couldn't seem to get enough of him. Every cell in my body screamed for his touch.

"Wait," he whispered, pulling back. When he bit his thumb and blood began to flow, I stared at it in wonder, unable to pull my gaze away.

"Drink from me," he whispered. "Live."

As I watched the red stream begin to slowly trickle down his hand, it seemed to call out to me, like an old friend. I licked my lips in anticipation of catching it on my tongue.

He kissed me again, but this time, all I could concentrate on was the smell of his blood. It was intoxicating and sweet.

"Butterscotch," I whispered as he pulled away and raised his hand to my lips.

"Don't be afraid," he said.

"Ethan," I moaned, feeling the heat build between my legs as the smell of his blood consumed me.

He rubbed his finger over my lips and sucked in his breath as I took it into my mouth.

"Oh…" I breathed, reveling in the sweet coppery taste. My legs began to tremble and the hunger inside of the pit of my stomach screamed for more.

"That's it," smiled Ethan as I began to suck greedily on his thumb. But it wasn't nearly enough and he knew it. The next thing I knew he held me down on the bed and placed his wrist over my mouth. "Do it," he demanded. "Break the skin. I'll be fine."

I closed my eyes and gave in to the ravenous hunger he'd created. Opening my mouth, I sunk my teeth into his skin until the blood began to spill, covering my lips and tongue. I lapped at the warm fluid and felt it go down my throat. I moaned against his wrist as a new kind of heat began to spread, from my face all the way down to the tips of my toes. With it grew a pleasure so intense, I wrapped my legs around him and pressed into his lap, this time wanting more than just blood.

"Nikki," he groaned, removing his wrist. He then tore my shirt away, exposing my naked body. "You're so beautiful," he murmured, staring down at my nudity.

"Your wrist," I whispered, as he began to lower his mouth to my breasts. "It's flowing much too freely."

He reached over and tore off a piece of the abandoned shirt and then wrapped it around the wound, stopping the blood.

"Now, it's your turn to be devoured," he said, his eyes full of flames.

I licked my lips, traces of his blood still lingering there. I wanted more, God did I want more of his blood, but I also wanted to feel his mouth all over my body again, like the other night.

As if he could read my thoughts, he began to touch me everywhere.

"Yes," I whimpered, as he cupped my breasts and began licking my nipples with his tongue, making me squirm.

"Say my name," he whispered, moving his fingers between my legs.

"Ethan…"

Soon, both of his hands and mouth were moving across my body, caressing and teasing my most sensitive spots, until I shuddered in ecstasy. Then he removed his own clothing and grasped my hand. "Touch me," he whispered, placing my hand on his chest.

His entire body was hard and muscular. When I reached down below and touched between his legs, he let out a strangled growl.

"What's wrong?" I asked as he pushed me away.

He shook his head and then spread my legs open. "I have to have you… right now," he said, pushing inside of me.

I wrapped my hips around his and moaned as he took me over the edge once more.

"May I?" he asked as he kissed the junction just above my shoulder.

"Yes," I whispered.

He opened his mouth and sunk his teeth into my neck, but there was no pain. For some reason, it only added to the ecstasy of his lovemaking, and soon he was unable to hold back.

"Nikki," he groaned, shuddering in pleasure inside of me. "God, I love you."

I stared up into his smoldering eyes and smiled. "I love you, too."

Just then, the bedroom door burst open and I heard a loud blast. Before I knew what was happening, Ethan's body slumped on top of me, pinning me underneath.

"Ethan!" I screamed, overwhelmed by the smell of blood and the fact he wasn't moving. Not at all.

"Got one of them," cackled an old man holding a shot gun. "Teach 'em for breaking in and sinning in our house."

In a flash, I shot out of bed and held the stranger up in the air by his throat. "What have you done?" I growled in rage.

The old man stared at me in horror, his watery brown eyes bulging out of his head as I began to squeeze the arteries in his neck.

"Let him go!" Hollered another man, standing in the doorway, his eyes full of shock. "Or I'll shoot!"

I glared at the guy, who looked like a younger version of the one I was choking. "I don't think so."

"Bitch, leave him be."

Something inside of me snapped as my eyes jumped back to Ethan's body. I wanted both men to pay.

"Killers," I choked, flinging the old man at his son. They both fell backwards to the floor and I advanced towards them.

"Shoot her," hollered the old man, trying to scramble away.

Before they could even blink, I had both of their guns and they were staring at me in horror.

"Run, Gabriel," barked the old man.

I grabbed the old man and surprising even myself, snapped his neck like a twig.

"Dad!" screamed the younger man, rushing towards us as I dropped his father.

"Stop!" I demanded, still stunned that I'd actually killed another human being so effortlessly.

But Gabriel grabbed me and punched me in the face, knocking me to the ground. "Demon!" he yelled. "I'm going to send you back to hell!"

"No!" I choked, standing up as he grabbed for his gun. I was faster, however, and seconds later, I had him down on the bed.

He screamed and tried pushing me away as I lowered my mouth to his neck. I sunk my teeth into his skin and began to drain the life out of him. Soon, he lay limp and I was able to finally relax my hold, savoring the sweet, tangy flavor of his blood. I felt the familiar heat spreading throughout my body and my thoughts returned, once again, to Ethan.

Ethan.

I could see him out of the corner of my eye and I began to choke on the other man's blood. I pushed him away and moved closer to Ethan.

"No," I moaned, staring in horror at the damage the bullet had inflicted on his head. Tears rolled down my cheeks as I studied him. I knew he could recover from wounds, but this seemed beyond any kind of resurrection. I held his face to my chest and sobbed, hoping beyond hope for some kind of a miracle.

We stayed that way for a long time and his skin grew so cool that I tried wrapping my body around him to offer heat. When that didn't work, I tore open my wrist and pushed it towards his mouth, hoping it would somehow draw him out and that maybe he'd miraculously wake up. But he didn't respond to that, either.

"Come back to me," I wept, touching his face with my fingertips. "Please come back to me."

I held him in my arms for what seemed like hours. When the sun went down and he still didn't wake up, I realized in horror that he really wasn't coming back.

Releasing a ragged sigh, I went into the closet and found a large pair of overalls and a white T-shirt. They practically fell off of my small frame, but I had no other choice.

"I will always love you, Ethan," I whispered somberly, kissing his cheek, wishing he'd suddenly raise his head and give me one of his sexy little smiles. But he didn't even twitch.

As a last resort, I ripped a piece of fabric from his shirt, tore open the old man's throat and dipped it inside, smothering it with blood. I then pushed part of the wet fabric into Ethan's mouth and let it rest there. It was a hopeless gesture, but I didn't know what else to do.

I walked to the door and turned back to look at him, one last time. "Goodbye," I whispered, before I eventually walked out of the room.

Chapter Twenty-nine

After cleaning some of the blood from my face and hair in the bathroom, I went outside and found an old truck parked next to the cabin, with the keys still in the ignition. I hopped inside and started the engine.

"Where the hell am I?" I mumbled, trying to find a way out.

The woods were dark but my eyes now seemed to adjust very well to nightfall. I quickly found the road and began driving, although I wasn't sure where in the hell I was even going. After driving north for a good forty-five minutes, I found a gas station and went inside. The moment I entered, the smell of pot and bubblegum engulfed my senses.

"Can I help you?" asked the stoned cashier who looked at me like I was some kind of freak.

I touched my face, wondering if I'd missed any blood. "Um, where am I?"

She smacked her gum and smiled. "You lost?"

I nodded.

She sighed and pushed a road map across the counter. "You're in Wolf Creek."

"Can I have this?" I asked, holding the map up.

She nodded. "Yeah, for five dollars."

"Well, can I at least just take a look at it?"

She shrugged. "Suit yourself."

I moved away from the counter and began studying the map. When I noticed I was only two hundred miles south of Shore Lake, I sighed in relief. I'd be home in less than three hours.

"Thanks," I told the girl, handing her back the map.

"Um, just keep it," she replied with a grimace, pushing it back towards me.

It was then I noticed the blood smudged on the paper. "Oh, sorry," I laughed weakly. "I... um hit a deer and had to push it off my vehicle. It was pretty gross."

"Bummer," she said, smacking her gum again. She then returned to some fashion magazine she was reading. When I got back into the truck, I looked at myself in the mirror and winced. I'd missed wiping the blood from my neck. I sighed and started driving.

***

When I finally made it back to Shore Lake, I went straight to the cabin, which had first appeared breathtakingly beautiful and serene but now appeared dangerously ominous. As I climbed out of the truck and approached the front porch, my stomach knotted up. My brother's car was now, surprisingly, parked outside of the cabin and I had no idea what was waiting for me inside. The realization that he might already be dead wasn't new to me, but it definitely was hard to swallow. I said a silent prayer and made my way up to the porch, trembling the whole way. As I got closer to the front door, I noticed it was slightly open.

Crap.

I placed my hand on the knob and took a couple of deep breaths before I finally had the courage to push it open. Of course it made a small creaking noise that seemed to echo more loudly than any gunshot I'd heard the past few days.

I stood in the entryway and was immediately met with an entourage of magnified smells – cedar, Pine Sol, and stale fruit. Fortunately, I didn't smell anything else, including blood.

I let out a sigh of relief and began searching the house. When I found nothing in the lower level, I walked upstairs to search the bedrooms and started with Nathan's, which was a mess. Clothes were strewn all over the place, someone had emptied out most of his drawers, and his model cars were broken and scattered. Someone had clearly done this in spite and anger. Seeing this mess added to my own rage.

I left his bedroom and searched my mother's, but didn't find anything unusual. My room was still a horrific mess, but I didn't seem to care about it anymore.

As I walked by my dresser mirror, I was again surprised to find an actual reflection, which looked pretty horrible at the moment. I seriously needed to get out of the dreadful clothes and clean up. I decided to risk a quick shower and then head over to Caleb's to see if I could find something that would lead me to my mother or Nathan.

I grabbed a towel and then jumped into the shower, washing my body as quickly as possible. As I rinsed the shampoo out of my hair, I thought of Ethan and my eyes welled up again. I still couldn't believe he was gone, killed by a simple shot to the head. I forced the image from my mind and finished up in the shower. When I was done, I wrapped the towel around my body and went back into my room.

"You're alive."

"Duncan!" I gasped, tightening my towel. "I thought you were dead!"

"Surprise, I'm not." He moved towards me and grabbed my arm. "Where is he?"

I shrugged him off. "Ethan?"

"Yeah, Ethan. Where's that bastard?"

I glared at him. "He's dead."

He laughed. "Right."

"He is dead!"

Duncan's eyes softened a little as he stared into my eyes. "I really thought you were dead, too," he murmured. "God, I was so worried about you."

I raised my chin. "Well, I almost died, thanks to you."

He frowned. "I had nothing to do with you getting shot. In fact, Ethan is the one who put you in danger, so don't blame me."

"Ethan is the one who saved my life. If it wasn't for him, I wouldn't be here."

His eyes moved to my neck and his face fell. "No… he turned you?"

I looked away and nodded. I was still having trouble accepting the fact that I was now one of them. I hadn't really wanted it, even if it had saved me from death.

He cleared his throat. "Have you fed yet?"

"Yes."

He sighed. "I'm sorry you had to go through that. But don't you see? These Roamers are the ones who've messed up all of our lives. Ethan dying is probably the best thing that could have happened."

I pushed him backwards. "Don't say that!"

He scowled. "He killed my father."

I shook my head. "No, they were lying to you, Duncan. It was either Caleb or Faye. I swear to God."

"But you don't know for sure," he said.

"I know that Faye is an evil, maniacal woman who will say or do anything to get her way."

He turned around and walked over to the balcony. "I guess I can't really argue that."

"Look," I said. "I need to get dressed and look for my family. I don't even know if they're still alive. Do you happen to know anything?"

Duncan turned around. "I think they're all in Vegas."

My eyes widened. "Alive?"

"I hope."

"And Nathan, too?"

He nodded. "Celeste came for him."

I released a sigh of relief. "Was he doing okay when she took him?"

"I think so."

I sat down on the edge of my bed and put my head in my hands. It was the first good news I'd had in a while. "Thank God."

"You have to get out of here, Nikki," he said. "Faye is still looking for you. If she finds you, she'll kill you."

I nodded. "Will you come with me to Vegas?"

He blew out a long breath and sat next to me on the bed. "I suppose. Someone's got to take care of you."

"Thank you," I said. "Wait for me downstairs?"

His eyes moved to my towel. "Are you sure you don't need help getting dressed?"

I sighed. "Duncan..."

His lips tightened. "You know, you should have been mine. We had something good going, and Ethan fucked it all up. Frankly, I'm glad he's dead."

"Duncan," I repeated, putting my hand on his forearm. Part of me still had feelings for him, but I wasn't ready to forget about Ethan. My blood still burned for him, even if he was gone. I couldn't just bury those feelings and move on. "We're good friends. Let's just keep it that way. I mean, I'm just so confused about everything right now."

He brushed my hand away and stood up. "I'll be downstairs."

I got up as he walked out of the bedroom and quickly slipped on a pair of jeans and a T-shirt. I then packed a duffel bag with more clothing and then went back into my mom's room to grab the money she'd been saving for Vegas. I stuffed it into my pocket and went back downstairs. When I met Duncan in the great room, he was sitting in the dark, staring into the unlit fireplace.

"You okay?" I asked.

"Peachy," he answered with a bitter smile.

I sighed. "Are you ready?"

He stood up and grabbed the duffel bag from me. "Have you flown yet?"

I shook my head. "I didn't like it when I was human. I'm sure I won't now, either."

"That may be so, but it's the quickest and cheapest way to get to Vegas. First, we'll need to feed, though, so we have enough energy."

Remembering the sweet taste of blood, my mouth watered. "I just fed a little while ago. I think I'm okay until we get to Vegas."

Plus, I wasn't sure if I could do it again. Doing it out of rage was one thing, but feeding on an innocent person was something entirely different. As far as I was concerned, it was still barbaric.

He sighed. "Fine. I'll wait, too."

I touched his cool cheek. "Are you sure you're going to make it? You feel cold."

"I'll be fine," he said, turning away. "Now, let's go."

We went outside into the fields behind the cabin.

"Now," he said, "it's time for a few "Vampire Life Lessons 101".

"I can't wait," I answered dryly.

He smiled. "Just be lucky you have me. I had to learn all of this on my own. It wasn't easy."

"Nothing about being one of these things appears to be easy," I said.

"Agreed. Now," he said, picking up a handful of snow and forming it into a ball. "You may notice that the climate won't affect you the same way as it used to. You won't necessarily be cold in sub-zero temperatures but the sun will no longer be your friend. So get used to staying out of direct sunlight and use sunglasses if you can't avoid being out during the day, or you'll be very uncomfortable."

"Okay."

He threw the snowball across the field, much farther than any normal person could. "We're insanely dexterous and fast."

I nodded. "So I've noticed."

"Watch this," he smiled.

In a blur, he was gone, but seconds later, he was back and holding a fluffy bear that had been on my bed.

I smiled and took it from him. "Okay, very impressive."

"Your turn, I want to see you move," he said.

I raised my eyebrows at the way he'd said it.

"What?" he chuckled. "I just want to see how fast you can go."

"Okay, but don't expect too much. I haven't had time to practice anything, you know?"

"It's pretty easy. Just concentrate on where you want to go and then start moving your legs."

"That easy, huh?"

"Yep. Go on," he urged.

I thought about the dock and began running. In less than two seconds, I was staring at the spot where I'd last seen Sonny, next to the boat house. I closed my eyes and shuddered.

"You okay?" asked Duncan, coming up behind me after a few seconds.

I cleared my throat. "So, where is he?"

"My dad?"

I nodded.

"I buried him," he answered, gruffly.

I touched his arm. "I'm so sorry, Duncan."

He stared out towards the lake. "I still can't believe it myself."

I motioned towards the lake. "My dad's out there."

He turned to me in surprise. "What?"

I nodded. "Celeste killed him. Ethan told me."

"What a surprise," he mumbled. "Ethan was around when your dad died."

"Ethan didn't kill my dad. He told me the truth."

Duncan sighed. "And of course, as always, you believed him."

"For the love of God, he didn't do it! I know it wasn't him. In fact, the night you were attacked and turned into a vampire, it wasn't Ethan, either."

His eyes widened. "Of course it was, we both saw him!"

I shook my head. "No, it was Faye. She's a shape-shifter! Don't you understand? She is the one who tried killing you! She wanted you to seek revenge on Ethan because of her own jealous, twisted mind."

"Why didn't she just kill him herself?"

I shrugged. "Who knows? The point is, Faye's dangerous and we have to find Nathan and my mom before she does."

He let out a long breath. "Okay, let's practice flying and then we'll go."

I nodded, very reluctantly.

"Someone's coming," he said, turning towards a pair of headlights in the distance. "We'd better hide."

I nodded.

He grabbed me and flew us up onto the roof of the cabin, where we both crouched down. As the vehicle moved closer I recognized Rosie.

"I wonder what she's doing here," I whispered.

"Probably looking for you. You've been gone for a couple of days and I think it's pretty safe to say you probably haven't filled her in on what's going on."

"I should talk to her. Maybe she knows something."

He grabbed my arm. "It's not a good idea. The less she knows, the safer she'll probably be."

I sighed and watched as Rosie got out of her car and walked up the steps to ring the doorbell. When nobody answered, she started back down the steps.

"What in the hell?" whispered Duncan.

I looked to where he was staring and my breath caught in my throat.

"That's impossible," I whispered in horror.

A lone man was walking out of the woods; his smile was one that I'd recognized growing up. It was a cold smile that meant trouble.

My father.

"It's my dad," I whispered.

Duncan stared at me in shock.

"I know," I mumbled. "Something's going on here."

"Can I help you?" hollered my dad, moving closer. He was dressed in the sheriff's uniform and looked more alive than I did at the moment.

Rosie turned towards him and I could tell she was more than a little taken aback. "Oh, I'm sorry – I was looking for Nikki!" she called back.

We watched as he moved closer to her. "I'm looking for her, too, as a matter of fact. She's missing, so are her brother and mother. You haven't seen any of them?"

Rosie shook her head and moved closer to her car. "No, I haven't. I'm sorry, have we met before?"

"I'm the new sheriff in town, Jim Smith," he lied, holding out his hand.

"Hello, I'm Rosie," she said.

Both of them were far away but my new senses caught their conversation as if I was standing there right beside them.

"So, you really haven't spoken to any of them?" he repeated.

She shook her head. "No, that's why I came out here. Nikki's missed work and hasn't returned my phone calls. That's not like her at all. As for her mom and brother, I haven't any idea where they are, either."

He sighed and stared out towards the road. "Well, I guess you won't be much help. But that's okay."

"What do you mean by that?" she asked in confusion.

The next thing I knew, he grabbed Rosie by the throat and twisted her neck, snapping it.

"Oh, my God!" I choked, as he tossed her body aside.

Duncan grabbed my hand tightly. "Shit, we have to get the hell out of here."

"You can come out now!" yelled my father, staring up towards us. "I know you're there."

I stared at Duncan in horror.

"It's not him," said Duncan.

"It is him," yelled my dad. "Now, both of you can come down here. I made dinner for you. Hurry before she gets too cold to enjoy."

I stood up and pointed towards him. "Who in the hell are you?" I screamed, tears rolling down my cheeks.

"Nikki!" growled Duncan, reaching for me.

"Ah…" smiled my father, a triumphant look on his face.

Before I knew what was happening, Duncan and I were flying through the forest, away from the cabin, as if we were faster than the speed of light.

Chapter Thirty

We landed clumsily, rolling in the snow.

"Shit, I'm sorry. You okay?" asked Duncan, helping me up.

I nodded and looked around. We were at the marina, inside of the fenced-in area where some of the boats were wrapped and stored.

"Duncan!" I screamed, as a shadow flew over our head.

He grabbed my hand and we began to run as our pursuer landed on the ground not far from us.

"It's pointless to run!" laughed my dad. "You can't escape me."

We jumped over the fence and soon we were speeding out of town again, with my dad still hot on our tails. When something grabbed my arm and pulled me back, I screamed in terror.

"Nikki," smiled my dad, holding me firmly by my shoulders. "Come on, that's no way to greet your father."

Duncan came back around and tried grabbing my dad by the back of the neck, but he was no match for him.

"Fool," he growled, releasing me. He turned to Duncan, grabbed him by the hair, and punched him in the face several times, sending him flying backwards with the force of the last one.

"No!" I choked, rushing towards Duncan, who was getting back up from the snow.

"So, where is he?" hollered my dad.

I turned to him. "Who?"

His smile was cold and evil. "Ethan."

I watched in wonder as his face and body began to change. Seconds later, we were staring at Faye, still dressed in the oversized sheriff's uniform.

"Ethan is gone," I snapped. "How did you find out about my dad?"

She shrugged. "It wasn't difficult. Now, what do you mean, Ethan is gone?"

"He's dead," answered Duncan.

She stepped closer and stared up at Duncan. "Dead? Don't tell me that you killed him?"

Duncan's lips thinned. "I didn't get the pleasure, but he is most certainly dead."

"Dead," she whispered hoarsely. "That can't be."

"It is," I said. "Someone shot him in the head."

Her face darkened. "It was your fault, you know. If you wouldn't have come back, he'd still be alive."

"I am not Miranda!" I hollered.

"Oh...but you can't fool me," she raged, spittle forming at the corner of her mouth.

"What in the hell do you want with us?" asked Duncan. "We've done nothing to you."

"You can leave," she told Duncan, still staring at me with a strange light in her eyes. "I have no quarrels with you."

"I'm not leaving without Nikki."

She turned to him and frowned. "Very well, then you'll die as well."

"There is no way in hell that I'll let you harm her."

"Fool," she spat.

Duncan tried grabbing my hand just as Faye pounced on him, knocking him flat to the ground. He kicked her and sent her flying backwards, but she recovered quickly. I stared in horror as she flew back towards him, her body changed, yet again, into the gargoyle-like creature I'd met in the woods the other night.

"Run!" hollered Duncan as he punched her in the face while she tried to rip his throat out with shark-like fangs.

"No," I choked, desperately trying to think of a way to help as they rolled around on the ground. I didn't want to get in the way, but I wasn't sure if he was strong enough to defeat her on his own.

"Fools," hissed Faye, grabbing him by the neck. "Nobody can escape from me."

"Run!" repeated Duncan as Faye's claws tore into the side of his face. I watched in horror as blood began to seep out of the wound and her long, black tongue reached out to taste it.

"Duncan!" I screamed as the touch of her tongue seemed to scorch his flesh.

He raised his face in pain and let out a deafening roar. Then, although in obvious agony, he grabbed her face with both hands, and somehow managed to pin her down. He raised his fist to punch her in the face just as her hand snaked up and slammed into his chest, sending him backwards. In a flash, she was on top of him again, slamming the back of his head against the ground. "Is that all you've got?" she rasped, her lips twisting into a triumphant smile.

I quickly moved behind her and grabbed her neck, which was actually very scaly and hard to hold onto.

"Bitch," she rasped, knocking me backwards with her elbow. She then jumped back off of Duncan, who was coughing and sputtering, and went after me.

"No!" I screamed, running away. Soon I was moving so fast that I felt as light as a feather. I imagined myself flying over the trees and before I realized what was happening, I actually was.

"Miranda!" raged Faye, coming up behind me. She grabbed my waist and both of us went tumbling down back towards the trees until we landed in a field of snow.

"Help!" I screamed, as she landed on top of me and held me down with her body.

She smiled in triumph. "You can't escape me," she said in a raspy voice. "Roamer or not. You're just weak and pitiful."

Just then I saw a flash of movement and Faye screamed out in anger as Duncan landed on her back and began beating the top of her head with his fists. She released her hold on me and grabbed one of his arms.

"Enough games," she growled, snapping his wrist. "Now, you will die." She hopped off of me, turned, and grabbed him by the neck, lifting him up into the air.

"Duncan!" I choked, trying to hit her so she'd let go.

"Oh, I do love the blood of a Roamer," she rasped.

Realizing what she was about to do, I jumped onto her back and began beating her with my fists.

But it was like beating on a steel door.

She knocked me down and then pulled his throat to her mouth, impaling him with her long fangs. I watched in horror as she ripped his throat apart, spraying blood all over the white snow.

"No!!!" I howled in anguish as his eyes rolled back into his skull and his body went limp. I jumped back onto her rough, scaly back and wrapped my hands around her reptilian throat. With all my might, I squeezed until she finally released Duncan.

"Your turn," she rasped, flying backwards. She slammed me back against a tree and I slid off of her.

"Oh..." I groaned in pain.

"Now," she said, turning around to stare down at me where I lay, trying to catch my breath. "This party is over."

I looked past her and my breath caught in my throat as I stared at the shadowed figure getting ready to pounce.

Faye attempted to turn around but it was too late, Ethan wrapped his hands around her throat, snapped her neck like a stick and then sunk his teeth into her scaly green skin. I watched as he drained her of all of her blood and then tossed her body aside.

"You're alive," I sobbed as he took me into his arms. "I can't believe it."

He kissed the top of my head and pulled me in tighter. "Thank God you are, too. Good thing I heard all the commotion when I was flying past."

"How did you make it?" I asked, looking into his ice blue eyes.

He stared down at me. "The bloody cloth you left near my mouth started the process. I wouldn't have survived if not for that."

It was then that I remembered Duncan. I pulled away from Ethan and ran over to where he lay, staring lifelessly up at the stars.

"Duncan," I choked, kneeling down next to his still form. There was so much blood running out of his neck and his cheek was ice cold. "Please don't die," I whispered, running my hand through his hair. I closed his eyes and kissed his forehead.

Ethan stood over us. "He won't die," he said. "If you can get him to feed."

I looked up at him. "How?"

Ethan sighed. "Open his mouth," he said.

I spread Duncan's lips apart and watched as Ethan knelt down next to us. He opened up his wrist and allowed his blood to trickle down to

Duncan's lips. "I can't believe I'm doing this," he said, squeezing his wrist to get more out.

"Thank you," I said.

"You can thank me later," he answered with a twinkle in his eye.

Duncan's eyes started to twitch, and within seconds, his throat began to form new patches of skin. Eventually, Ethan was able to place his wrist against Duncan's mouth and he was able to feed on his own.

"I can do it if you're getting too weak," I said to Ethan, who appeared to grow paler by the second.

Ethan shook his head. "Nobody is feeding from you," he said gruffly.

Duncan's eyes slowly opened and he stared in confusion at Ethan. "No," he mumbled, pushing his wrist away.

"Duncan, don't be like that. Ethan just saved your life," I whispered. I noticed that most of the wound on his neck was already healed when he stood up.

"Where is she?" he asked, his voice hoarse.

"Dead," I said, motioning towards Faye's body.

"Are you sure about that?" asked Duncan, stumbling toward it. "Apparently, being dead around here doesn't last."

Ethan laughed. "It's a good thing for you."

Duncan turned to him. "Is it?"

Ethan rolled his eyes.

"You need more blood," I said to Duncan.

He bent forward and spit out some kind of bloody phlegm. "Yeah," he agreed. "I suppose I do. What then?"

"Well, I'm still going to Vegas to search for my mom and brother," I answered.

"You still want my company?" asked Duncan.

"She won't need it now," piped in Ethan. "But thanks, anyway."

"Of course you can come," I said, ignoring him. "That is, if you'd still like to."

Duncan nodded. "Yeah, I would. Nathan's my friend, too."

"Swell," muttered Ethan under his breath.

"We should all feed," said Duncan, moving towards the woods. "We need the strength for travel."

I sighed. "Yeah, I'm pretty weak myself. What about you, Ethan?"

Ethan nodded. "Same here. So, where should we dine?"

Duncan turned around and a small smile formed across his face. "Club Nightshade?"

Oh, God... not that place.

"I... I don't think I can," I said, rubbing my forearm.

Ethan put an arm around my shoulders and guided me towards Duncan, who was waiting for us at the edge of the woods. "In order to live, you have to learn how to feed, like it or not, Nikki. But don't worry; I'll be at your side to show you how."

I let out a long breath and then nodded. I'd do whatever it took to find my brother and mom. Nothing would hold me back.

End of Book Two

Now Available

***

Made in the USA
San Bernardino, CA
03 February 2015